Beerjacket

Silver Cords

Songs and stories

Silver Cords. Songs & Stories.

ISBN: 978-1-5272-2929-7

Stories, songs and illustrations by Peter Kelly 2018
All rights reserved.

Released & Published by Scottish Fiction. Catalogue no: SF014
Book design by Julia Doogan, juliafrancesdesign.co.uk
First printed in 2018 by Claro Print, claroprint.co.uk
With funding help from Creative Scotland, creativescotland.com

To Clare, Luke and Gemma

You were always on my mind
You are always on my mind.

Preface

THIS ALBUM IS FILLED to the brim with time. So many moments, hours, months and years live in it that to hear it now is like watching myself ageing in a mirror of sounds, ideas and stories. But for me, that has made it a thing separate from time and more than just a document of connected moments. It has captured points of my life in flux, a series of detached moments stitched together like patchwork.

Officially, I started writing the album in 2015 (although I was visited after that by an old ghost from much longer ago) and I imagined it would all fall into shape by the end of that year. I was completely wrong. It was two years on before the recording had been fully completed and had it not taken so long, a quarter of the songs would have been missing from the final album. At the time of writing, I'm still months away from being finished with this project. There is an irrational part of me that wonders if I will ever actually sign off on this as a completed body of work. But then it's always this way, even with a more traditional record than this one. You doubt yourself, you doubt the songs, you doubt the time of year, you doubt the world. I think that doubt is the main component that influences any creative work. From the earliest point in the process, you doubt that you're going the right way and you constantly think and rethink. Eventually, you decide that the only thing you can be sure of is that this is terrible and you have made a tremendous mistake in believing otherwise.

At some point in the writing of the album, I decided the record would live in a book and that each song would be accompanied by a short story inspired by its lyrics. My friend, Kristin Hersh, has been releasing albums in a book format for years now and I was inspired by her (as I always am) but I always need to make things as difficult for myself as possible, which led me to write fiction rather than personal essays. I continuously put myself through the wringer.

And here's the thing: I don't assume for a moment that the result of all of this work will be that everyone will drop what they're doing to fall at its feet. The result of all of this work will be that I made this thing exist outside of my head and that's enough.

The songs for this record aside, the album wouldn't exist as it does without others' contributions and support.

Stuart MacLeod, who recorded the album, has been a friend for over twenty years. Over the past eight years, he has been recording studio albums with me that far surpass anything I could have accomplished alone.

Technically, Silver Cords took two years to record but the truth is that the time actually recording could have fit inside a month. Most of the time between sessions was filled with real life and work on other projects along with the waiting, the frustration, the not-knowing and the writing and rewriting, without which this record would have been a different record. So much time is contained now in the album that it's all the more precious to me. Now it's a time capsule in which there are words rather than objects to remind me of how I felt along the way. There are sounds from one day alongside sounds from another year. Errors (good and bad) hundreds of days apart sit smirking together like brothers and sisters in a family photograph. I'm the parent of all of this, and I love it, but I still try to pose it to make it beautiful to others.

One of the best things about working with Stuart over the past few years, and especially on Silver Cords, is that he has made me take a step back and allow things to happen. There were whole years when I was working on this album without owning copies of the recordings. If I'm honest, there were times when I didn't even feel sure there was an album. I knew there were songs but despite the hours of recording, I had no way to hear what we'd been doing. In the end, this was best as without the necessary separation from the recordings, I would have been inclined to 'fix' any quirks or idiosyncrasies. Doing so would have removed the uniqueness of what we had captured and Stuart is wiser than me in knowing the difference between a mistake and a moment. When the mixes began arriving in my inbox night after night, after such a long time of working and waiting, I was reunited with all of those hours. I felt rich with time in a way that I would never have appreciated had I not been forced to wait for the moments to arrive.

I remember the first time I heard Julia Doogan sing. She and her band had been booked to play with me almost ten years ago in Edinburgh and on hearing her, the thought that occurred to me then was the same one I have had every time since: how does she make her voice cut through every other noise? It's truly one of the purest sounds I've ever heard. She has greater control than me by far and the way she glides from one note to another is so naturally graceful, throwing each nuance of a melody around like a beachball.

The paradox in her case is that she recorded all of her vocals in one day yet she is partly responsible for the tardy completion of this project as she insisted it would be more special if I did all of the artwork myself. She's right though, a concept like one this requires a certain amount of singularity if the vision is to be fully realised. Nevertheless, it's hard not to be frustrated with myself that all of this is in my head and I haven't been able to work faster to finish it earlier. When I read all of this back later and factor in the frustration I have felt up until now, maybe I'll be able to understand better why all of this time spent in suspended animation was necessary.

The final piece of the jigsaw is Neil Wilson, who is releasing the record as a book through his appropriately-titled Scottish Fiction label, having never previously released a record as a book before. When you are tempted to take a bold step which you fear might take you off a cliff, it's important to find someone in your world who will give you that encouraging shove, should you at any point be tempted to back off and decide that potentially walking off of cliffs might not be a great idea. Meet Neil. We've worked together many times over the years and I had been really impressed by the records he was releasing through his label. When he offered to release Silver Cords, I told him I wanted to put it out it as a book of short stories, fully expecting him to throw in his cards at the suggestion. Not so. He has supported this project throughout its difficult birth and I'm very grateful to him for sticking with it, especially as working with me on this has often simply meant waiting for me.

Fortunately, my songs have always been born without much of a struggle but the stories did not immediately arrive so naturally, particularly as my idea was for the stories to be short enough to be read alongside the corresponding song as it played. And that is almost certainly not the case, unless you are a remarkably fast skim-reader. Each idea about this album seemed to be born out of a self-defeating desire to destroy my own work. Again, as I write this sentence, this thing is still incomplete and, to be absolutely honest, I often experience flashes of anxiety around this project. Firstly: this is so far from finished that I have no idea when it will be done. Secondly: if I keep having new ideas, it will actually become impossible to ever truly accept that it is finished. Thirdly: I fear that no one will ever know or care about this piece of work anyway.

Maybe I shouldn't admit to these fears but withholding them does nothing to protect me from them.

Story by story, approximately once a month, the songs' siblings entered the room. My imagination has superimposed details on the real-life buildings that inspired settings and, in some way, the stories play out there interminably now on three to five minute loops. People who don't live live there and some have blood on their hands. Others are invisible beneath their suits and the birds that fly above the town carry a man cut out from the photos of his family. The elderly wake up as children and houses are disappearing.

The stories are alive all around me. They've left a trail mapping out where they were born, where they lived and where they rested. Sometimes in planned sittings in coffee shops, sometimes in notes in transit from one place to another, sometimes midway through conversations. It's hardly surprising then that the stories are everywhere.

After such a long process, it's funny to think that I'm getting closer, day by day, to finishing. I can at last, or at least, acknowledge that it will be at an end soon and that eyes other than my own will be reading it.

Foreword | *Last Songs*

MAYBE WE ARE LIVING in the last days of physical things. Maybe we are the last of those physical things.

Everything now seems to exist in some vague realm that we pin down weakly with language that is itself constantly evolving and morphing. We don't really possess anything anymore, we only access and share things. We're all just floating in space. Of course, we always were just floating in space but now, without any objects to weigh us down, it feels like we could just spin off into orbit and lose the illusion of being anywhere.

When I was growing up, I cared more about records and books than pretty much anything else. For that very reason, I owned barely any records or books because these things had value and with value, there was always a cost. Now we struggle to convince people that things have a value at all and no-one wants to pay for anything. Maybe as well as living in the last days of physical things, we are living in the days of the last songs. People who care for songs beyond their three minutes are a dying breed.

The first time you heard a song used to be carved into your memory, entwined with other firsts and vital seconds. A song was like the DeLorean from Back To The Future. Hearing a song could transport your atoms immediately to a different time and place like you had stepped through a portal, a magical mirror.

These days the only things people will readily pay for are those which offer convenience or which have some sort of practical usefulness. Well, art isn't convenient at all and it's fiercely impractical but there can be no doubt of its deep and essential value. Without art, we couldn't hope to express the world of dreams and instead we would be stuck with the cold and monochromatic routine of the everyday. In dreams and in art, you can be anywhere, do anything, be anyone.

Dreams are the cords sewn throughout our realities. If yours are as vivid as mine, they might be more tangible than many real things anyway. How many times have you woken up to find yourself facing a new morning and wondered, what on earth is going on? For however many hours you manage a night, you are repeatedly immersed in what you are sure is real only to find that it was not.

That state of disorientation is one in which most of us secretly live our lives, pretending all the while that we know exactly what we are doing and understand fully what the world expects of us. The truth is that everyone is guessing but some of us happen to be gifted actors (or just liars) and those are the very people whose apparent lack of fear places so much pressure on the rest of us to be sure of our direction.

So, in this time of floating impermanence, the act of buying a book or a record really feels like a grand gesture. Like picking a side. The side that says that art matters. The one that says no to practical things in favour of the practice of things. It's a team to which anyone can belong because there is a book, a record, a photograph or a painting that will seem to speak louder to you than anyone else in the universe. Even better is the realisation that there may be millions of others who feel the same way about that same work of art as you do. For each of those people, it is a mirror of something true to them as individuals and simultaneously it connects them to all of those other individuals. No-one is alone and no-one is completely unique. Imagine if we all stopped and looked up to see ourselves in each other and just listened together. We would still be floating in space without a clue what we are doing, but how much better would it be to join hands and float together?

Now imagine we had real physical things again.
Imagine the weight that would give us.
Those things that we used to love and be defined by.
Imagine that we tied ourselves to those mirrors again, the ones that allow us to see ourselves, to be ourselves and to be with others.

Nervous | *Lift*

Nervous

The dream of you hangs like a scared caught fish
The hook is through but the heart is prone to wish
All night my head sinks.

I have given my best: a solid seven out of ten
But when you cast the net, I am a carp among men
And I'll swim upstream
I'll swim upstream.

My eyes don't close at night
There's a flashing light beneath the surface
Time just melts like ice
While the windows yawn behind the curtains
The tide begins to rise
I feel the weight lift from me
But it just makes me nervous
It just makes me nervous.

You put the song of the sea in my head
And I drift for miles but never reach my bed
All night my head swims.

I never rest, I move continuously
And I repeat these same mistakes habitually
And I'll forgo sleep
I'll forgo sleep.

Peter Kelly – vocal, guitar, ukulele
Stuart MacLeod – pump organ

THIS IS THE SONG OF THE SEA.

It can sometimes feel as if you're drifting through life, not directionless but being directed by some other force outside of your own control. The fear that powerlessness can bring is counterbalanced by the freedom of accepting you are just a passenger.

I have a strange relationship with dreams. For me, there is only a very thin membrane between reality and the world of dreams. I often feel I live in the parasomniac space between sleeplessness and hypnogagia, the exploding head place where your senses shake themselves into waking with a jolt like a starting pistol.

————

Lift

SAMUEL HAD BEEN AWAKE for twelve whole days. Physically, he was now absolutely dead on his feet and his eyelids felt as if they were lined with sandpaper. His tongue was alien in his mouth, dry and sour. His mind was gradually unravelling and he was in a constant state of fright, disorientation and delusion. Every moment shocked him. Each second was a horror.

Throughout the first days, he had jumped at sounds leaking into reality from the starved dreams his waking usually kept at bay. Occasionally, he would be surprised by the emergence of a sudden surge of laughter exploding from his own mouth, rising like an urgent bubble from the bottom of a tank. He could retain nothing he saw or heard in his memory for more than a minute. Never would he have been described as an intelligent man before the insomnia, but now he seemed incapable of processing or storing even the most straightforward information. Facts passed through him like ghosts of the waking world.

However, the relative strangeness of his initial experience of sleeplessness was a world away. More than having peered into the void between sleeping and waking, he now lived there permanently and he could no longer imagine returning to the state of normalcy in which he had lived before.

Samuel had been a champion weightlifter, picking up incredible mass and national prizes, but those days were a thing of the past. As he aged, he had been more and more frequently overtaken by the younger, hungrier men. He knew that his next event was likely to be his last. He felt that to fail would be worse than death. To be an ex-champion is a greater sorrow than never to have won.

Initially, he had rationalised his sleeplessness as a symptom of nerves in the lead-up to the big event, which was understandable as he had not been hitting the mark for quite some time. After a few restless hours, he would just get up and train again to make use of the time he would otherwise have spent fighting with himself to sleep.

Though he knew sleep was essential for the growth of his muscles, his body seemed to be telling him otherwise. Incredibly, he found he could lift more weight and for longer, the less time he slept. He was lifting two and three times the weight he could before and he was heavier, too. When he looked in the mirror, he did not always recognise the man staring back at him.

Other people had begun to notice the changes in him and their reactions ranged from concern to delight. His mother was beside herself with worry but his manager looked at Samuel like a winning lottery ticket. This story was gold-dust. At worst, it was a car-crash everyone would want to witness; at best, it would be a testament to his superhuman indestructibility. By a perverse instinct, many members of the public hoped Samuel would go completely mad. The more successful others are, the more pleasure we take in their failure. Each time the story was shared on social media, it was supplemented by the individual's own opinion, projection or thesis. When something like this happens, it seems that everyone feels entitled or expected to commentate, believing that the world awaits their take.

There were inevitably rumours of drug use but clean test after clean test silenced his accusers. This was a phenomenon, plain and simple. The event was big news and the newly-christened 'Sleepless Sam' was odds-on to clear the board.

But Samuel's paranoia grew with each day. He read all of his own press and soaked up all the public opinions, which mixed with the voice of doubt in his own mind. He would sporadically scream out obscenities and throw his hands at invisible enemies.

The eyes of the media remained fixed on him around the clock on a live twenty-four hour news channel, beaming his relentlessly wakeful state to an eager world. What had started as a private revelation had become a global curiosity. And still his strength grew day by day, the more starved he was of sleep. As a champion weightlifter, he was stronger than most men who had ever walked the earth, but now manic energy burst through him like a ferocious riptide of inspiration and anger. Surges of electrical activity shocked his every movement and overloaded his body with primal animation.

In his final days, all expression had left his wrought face. He looked like an abandoned building, derelict and haunted. When he spoke (which was seldom, few thoughts appeared to pass through his head) he would slur as if drunk, his cadence a dull monotone. A press conference was abandoned by management midway through as his responses to even the most straightforward questions were alarmingly incoherent. By this point, the macabre interest of the press and the public in Samuel's unravelling had spun out of control; best to deny them their feeding frenzy.

His manager spoke into Samuel's blank face and he felt he could hear the words reverberate around his empty head. "This has gone far enough, Sam. What could possibly be left to prove?"

Samuel stared through and beyond him at the light that appeared evermore frequently in his vision. A colossal brightness that spread across his eyes and enveloped the world like fire. The light had first arrived during sleep, just prior to the insomnia setting in, bursting behind his eyelids and rousing him as if his bedroom was ablaze. Now, the luminescence was ever-present and made everything glow like neon. When Samuel looked at his reflection, the light was all around him and he shone like a halo in a religious painting.

On his twelfth night awake, Samuel revealed his light to the world.

There, live onscreen, his otherworldly radiance was so discernible that people in their living rooms across the globe simultaneously adjusted their television sets in vain. He shone like a celestial body and the halo around him seemed to pulse like a heart.

All of a sudden, Samuel's eyes widened and his face started with a shock. What he remembered or realised at this moment, no-one will ever really know for sure. The light now burst forth from him with a new intensity such that all the eyes on all the televisions all over the world were forced to close. It was like a crushing sleep had collapsed the eyelids of mankind in one simultaneous blink.

When the eyes warily opened, Samuel was gone from sight.

At first, confusion seemed to freeze the world as it watched, then all of a sudden, there was blankness. The station rushed to the commercials and an advert filled the screen for Lift, a fish oil-based insomnia treatment.

Maybe when you fall under the weight of the waves of your dreaming, you're really lifting, not the waves but yourself, high above your head.

Maybe dreaming is the punchline to a joke about waking.

Forest | *The Loneliest Places*

Forest

There's a fiction stuck in your teeth
On your black tongue's affection that you don't believe
You're an empty hall that echoes conceit
In an abandoned building that burns and it bleeds
A screaming forest of falling trees
No clouds move for you when your clown lungs breathe
A dream is real when you're asleep but you're not here.

Without direction, you direct the scene
If you were young, you would be living beyond the screen
You're fickle and you're fake and you flee
You abandon anything when it wakes up real
A screaming forest of falling trees
No clouds move for you when your clown lungs breathe
A dream is real when you're asleep but you're not here.

People's faces are just faint traces
All your dreams now are just blank spaces
Constant status of constant stasis
You're a map of the loneliest places.

Peter Kelly – vocal, guitars, footstomp

There's a meanness to this song which I might feel ashamed of
if it wasn't directed towards myself.

But it's probably directed at you too. We're becoming
increasingly detached as people. We invite loneliness culturally in
a way that differentiates us from our ancestors. The social nature
of our character is morphing and any remnants of that element
of human nature probably live mostly in the digital ether. We
are being increasingly denaturalised as a species and looking at
screens more often than we look through windows.

We're so steeped in the artifice of the modern world that
even when we make genuine attempts to communicate, they
are hijacked by beeps alerting us to another conversation, our
pockets and wrists vibrating with something like life that is
nothing like life.

Youth is often described as ignorant but that's not fair, youth
is only learning. Real ignorance is learned through the experience
that stops you listening. The real shame isn't in not knowing
better, it's in thinking you know better. When you believe you've
found the answers, then you're really lost.

———————

The Loneliest Places

JOE WAS GONE. For fifty years, Aisling had parted with him only when they put the day to sleep and together they had welcomed each new morning in the same bed in the same room in the same house.

Their house was one of many in a terraced block of terraced blocks but it was their house, and in that way, it was unique – the most special place in the world. Its walls had breathed in the words they had spoken to each other for so long that they reverberated with the sounds of their life together. Hanging there in photographs from decades back were ghosts of times before, smiling out of glass, fixed in moments of their happiness.

It had always been just the two of them. Children had never arrived. For some years, that was the only loss she had lamented in her life, followed later by the deaths of her parents, then her friends, and now Joe.

Now Joe was gone.

Her mother had been a tall lady, so tall with such long limbs that at first you might not even have noticed that she was beautiful, or at least quite how beautiful she was, when she entered a room. It was as if her height was the fact and her being beautiful was an idea you'd think of later. Nevertheless, her father never let a day go by without telling whoever was there to listen that she was the most perfect woman he had ever seen.

In Aisling's memories, her mother always wore the same red dress. Frills decorated the bust, sleeves and skirt like smiles. As time went on, Aisling came to realise that the omnipresence of the dress was more likely her memory's simplification of the past. Even if she had only worn the dress once or twice, it had made such an impression on her that Aisling had superimposed it onto every moment of her life. In memories, we see the things we love through the most flattering filter.

They made a funny looking pair, her mother and father. He was almost a foot shorter than her but quite the most masculine man you could imagine, his testosterone levels spelled out in curlicues of thick black hair. He might have looked quite a frightening character except for the smiles tucked inside the creases that lined his eyes. He loved her mother with a furious passion so intense it inspired Aisling's own romanticism of the idea and the pursuit of love.

But the longer you live, the more you lose, and losing Joe was worst of all.

They had met at a dance in the town. He was some dancer, Joe. She was clumsy and could never quite slot into the rhythm, always preferring to watch at the side until he took her in his arms and swept her up in the music until she felt like she was in water, as if she was being guided like a fish acquiescing to the undertow. Unlike her squat and square-bodied father, Joe was tall, lean and sinewy with muscles like gobstoppers punctuating his limbs. She would fall into his arms and let them push and pull her around the floor like that magical sweeping brush from Fantasia. It was such a pleasure for her to just relinquish all power over her body when he danced her around the hall.

She had shared more time with that man than she had with any other person in the world. His life and hers were intertwined as one cord, not two lives at all but one. As they lowered him into the grave, she felt as if the ground was swallowing her, too.

Her next door neighbour brought her home in the afternoon once everyone else had left the wake. Catherine was her name. She wasn't a close neighbour, at least not in the way neighbours used to be close. Back when Aisling first moved here all those decades ago, neighbours were your friends and really more like family. They were all gone now and most were dead. She was the last remnant of that old community.

Catherine had knocked on the door a few days before to see if she could help with anything. She had noticed the ambulance arrive and twitched at her curtain to watch as Joe was stretchered out of the house, Aisling shaking and moaning behind him.

After giving her a hug at the door and making her a cup of tea, Catherine was leaving to pick up her kids from school. "Remember, you can phone me if there's anything I can do for you," she said, scribbling her number on the newspaper in the hall, now four days out of date.

Aisling closed the door and turned around to face the mirror in the hall. Look at that old lady, she thought. Look at the candyfloss hair, the sunken cheeks, the stretched face trapped in the wax of her skin.

She fell asleep collapsed in her chair while the tea lost its heat beside her.

Soon a fiction was enveloping her and she felt as if she was being parachuted into the past. Joe had never believed her when she'd say she didn't dream.

"Aisling, you just don't remember them," he'd say.

With her eyes closed and her mind spilling its imaginings, she found she was no longer alone in the room. She was surrounded by all of those old friends and neighbours, family in all but blood, encouraging the loosening of her tears as they stroked her hands and gave soft sympathetic sounds to her ear.

More cups of cold tea congregated as the dream went on, periodically produced by one neighbour after another, each whispering in her ear and squeezing her hands until the tears came. This looped in her brain until she became conscious of another presence in the room. Joe.

"Why are you crying, Aisling?"

She searched for him through the blur of her tears until gradually he was revealed, crouching beside her with his hand solid on her shoulder. Grief was tied in the moment of her joy and she kept touching her hand to his hand as it rested upon her before she became satisfied that this was real. Words wouldn't come, all that made sense was touch.

Aisling suddenly realised that everyone else had gone and that she and Joe were alone in the living room. Another wave crashed upon her. They were gone again. Just as soon as she had received Joe's return, she faced again the painful loss of her friends.

"They're gone again," she said.

"They're dead, Aisling. They've all been dead for years."

She looked up to meet his eyes and realised that she knew this already. There was a smile in the corner of Joe's left eye, a banana-shaped crease that she'd always loved. Holding his hand tightly in her bony grip, she realised something else but fear trapped the words inside of her mouth. Joe nodded as if to say, go on and let it out. Aisling shook her head frantically like a child refusing a hated meal. Joe tipped his head to one side and smiled sympathetically before nodding again. Still, Aisling shook her head and pressed her eyelids together to shut out the threat of the moment.

"Aisling," Joe said quietly, "You know I'm not here either."

She pulled away from him and put her hands over her ears, keeping both eyes firmly closed.

"Aisling, did you hear me? I'm not here."

He repeated this over and over and she clamped her hands tighter over her ears to try to block him out, or at least to attempt to block out the cruelty of this cold, cold truth. To be in this room in their precious home where they had shared their lives together and to hear him telling her that he was gone? No, no, not this. Not again. This was the loneliest place, she was sure, there could be none lonelier. She was sure this was the loneliest place, this must be the loneliest place.

The sound of her mother's voice leaked into her brain and brought her floating out of sleep into the loud reality of a warm summer afternoon, children playing in the street outside and sunlight flooding the room, filtering through a doll's auburn hair as she posed frozen on the windowsill.

"Aisling," her mother said. "Aisling, did you hear me?"

Behind her mother's giant red-dressed body was a long curved mirror hanging on the wall. She looked deeply into the eyes of the little girl in the glass. The eyes were too big for her body and there was a comical halo of hair rising from the back of her head, filled with static from the pillow.

At the sight of the little girl, her lip vibrated and she exploded like a shaken bottle of lemonade. Her mother held her steady in her long skittle arms as the bowling ball of the truth came rushing towards her. She held fast to her. There is no greater protection you can find than the love of a mother. The rocking took hold of her pain like an anaesthetic. Aisling even allowed her eyes to close over, feeling her grief begin to float away. Before she fell fully to sleep, she came to in a burst of memory and a scream tore from her as if in the throes of childbirth, her loss reborn.

"Aisling," her mother said. "Did you hear me? I'm here."

There in her mother's attempts to comfort her echoed Joe's agonising last words, spinning around and around, making her feel as if she was being turned again by him on that dancehall floor. There were the black words, spoken in her husband's gentle and beautiful voice, repeating like the stuttering punches of graveside raindrops, the accidental cruelty of the truth, the worst cruelty of all.

"Aisling, did you hear me? I'm not here."

"Aisling, did you hear me? I'm here."

"Aisling, did you hear me? I'm not here."

She watched in the mirror as her mother held the little girl. She kept repeating his name like a curse or a prayer. Her mother stroked her hair and shushed her softly, making a rhythm of the undulating slither of the sounds as they grew and died, breathing through her teeth.

Before and after: the loneliest places.

Everybody's Song | *How It Feels To Fear*

Everybody's Song

I think today's a day when things get broken
Punished just for being here
I think today's a day when truths are spoken
It's funny how it feels to fear
I drink too much poison and it leaves me choking
My tongue swollen up like a spear
I sink like a shipwreck from a nightmare woken
Sudden as the iceberg nears

I'm tired of hearing my own voice

You know you're doing it all wrong
If you're singing someone else's song
But then you knew that really all along
So you tried writing everybody's song
You tried righting everybody's wrongs.

I shrink with rage and all the bitter passions
Vanishing from the inside out
Blink and you'll miss me as I pass from fashion
The past has passed without doubt

I'm tired and I don't have a choice

You know you're doing it all wrong
If you're singing someone else's song
But then you knew that really all along
So you tried writing everybody's song
You tried righting everybody's wrongs.

There's an echo racing round the room so empty
Here's the silence you complained was never yours
Where are the faces that reflected you exist now?
Why did you want the sickness and never the cure?

You know you're doing it all wrong
If you're singing someone else's song
But then you knew that really all along
So you tried writing everybody's song
You know you're doing it all wrong
If you're singing someone else's song
But then you knew that really all along
So you tried writing everybody's song
You were right and everyone was wrong.

Peter Kelly – vocals, guitars, mandolin
Stuart MacLeod – shaker
Julia Doogan – vocal

SINGING SOMEONE ELSE'S SONG might mean doing whatever another person wants you to do at the expense of your own freedom.

The day this song appeared was one of those when you just feel crushed by everything. The details of that day (or any other bad day) don't really matter but that feeling is one worth trapping like a wasp in a jar.

When you capture that feeling, you can watch it throwing itself against the glass walls, fizzing and frugging with its malevolent passions. Asking why bad days happen is as futile as asking why there are wasps. Wasps feed their babies with insects that would harm your plants. Just like that, a bad day destroys the things that would harm your creativity. Boredom. Complacency. Maybe even happiness. Sometimes you need to lose these things to create.

———

How It Feels To Fear

It's FUNNY HOW SOME days smack of impending doom.

On those days, you wake up with what feels like a pre-hangover. That is, you wake up with the fear of what will be rather than what was. What's more, on days like those, you aren't even responsible for the horrors ahead so you can't prepare the apologies that would begin the repairs. On days like those, you can only ready yourself for the downpour of grief and face the fact: you're going to get wet.

Maybe right now you are thinking back to one such day when you were acutely aware of that fear-before-the-fear. Maybe you woke up this morning with the feeling that today will be another one. To remember those days feels almost like tempting fate. It feels like you're goading the universe in acknowledging that they ever happened as if to say, come ahead, what else do you have for me?

It was on a day like this that I lost my shoes.

Okay, we've all had days when an item disappears and you waste inordinate time searching for it. The frustration and the panic of the experience brings equal parts exasperation and perspiration. There's a ridiculous rage underneath it all that this is some cruel joke orchestrated by God or the universe. Some omnipotent being is laughing at you with your shoes in its hands. The truth is that in some way you're really hiding the shoes from yourself.

To make matters worse, on this particular morning, I absolutely had to leave the house immediately as I was already running late for an important meeting at the start of the day. If I arrived late, I would look foolish. If I arrived late with no shoes on, I would look even more foolish. Wearing another pair of shoes wasn't an option either as at that time I only had two pairs: the lost ones and slippers. Wearing slippers to a meeting definitely wouldn't do.

I looked in each room, muttering and cursing as I went, and quickened my movement across the house as I searched like I was trying to catch them out before they could run to another hiding place. My anger didn't help, fizzing impotently and making no impression on my situation or on the universe that I was sure had caused it.

I called my wife and asked her if she had seen my shoes.

"Yes, David," she said, "I saw them on your feet yesterday."

She might have thought that this was a funny response but at this point I couldn't see any comedy in my situation, even if it didn't quite cut it as tragedy.

Looking at the clock, it was now clear that there was no way I was going to make the meeting, not given the half-hour commute and the fact that my feet were covered only in socks. Ironically, my 'Tuesday' socks, which might have made me appear to be perfectly organised for the day ahead, despite the fact I was neither wearing shoes or aware of where they were in my house.

And it was Thursday.

I already knew what everyone at work thought about me (erratic, careless, a liability) and the last thing I wanted was to add to the list of flaws I felt sure they were compiling behind my back. Eventually, my head would be on the chopping block and I'd have no-one but myself to blame. Still, I'd hate them for it all the same. In some ways, it would be a relief when they finally told me I could stay at home in my socks for as long as I wanted.

I can't explain why but whenever I become stressed, I make up songs to calm my nerves. For most, a song comes out of the radio but for some, a song will come from their heads and that's my experience. Whilst a song is sung and heard, I think the truest of them are never really written at all. A real song just breathes itself into life and the best of them outbreathe their writers. I believe that every song that has ever existed has always been there floating in the air waiting for someone to come along and say, "This one's mine." A song appearing in my mind feels like walking into a cobweb. When that happens, I always feel like there's some of it still stuck to me.

As I searched and failed, I found myself singing.

"I think today's a day when things get broken…"

A melody had formed around the moment and all of a sudden, everything felt somehow okay. Rather than continue to try to find my shoes, I simply sat down on the bed again and began to peel back the first of my socks. When I did so, it became immediately clear that my plans were about to change. Not only today but for good.

There was no foot beneath the sock.

I breathed in sharply and a wash of tears came rushing to my eyes. My chest tightened and a smir of sweat covered my face. I kept looking away in an attempt to compose myself before checking again, growing dizzier and fainter until I finally slipped completely out of consciousness and fell crashing to the floor.

On coming to, I felt the carpet burning my skin and the unmistakable sensation of a bruise forming along the right side of my face.

I lifted my head to look at the LED display on the alarm clock. 9:10. No need to rush now, the meeting would be over by the time I arrived, if I ever actually managed to leave the house. Steadying myself with my arms on the bed, I pulled my body into a sitting position and looked down again at the bizarre sight of my missing foot and my 'Tuesday' sock. The strangest thing was that I could still feel the foot I could clearly see was absolutely not there. I pulled off the other sock to find that it too was empty but this time, I didn't feel faint or surprised or even scared. Actually, I felt strangely free.

Lifting myself onto my two invisible feet, I looked at the mirror and found exactly the sight I expected to see. My clothes all looked as they normally would but where I would usually be met by my face, neck and hands, there was absolutely nothing there.

As I stood up on my two non-feet and stared at this impossible sight, my mobile phone began to ring in my pocket. I lifted it out with an invisible hand and saw the screen flash up the office number. Of course, my boss would be furious and demand an explanation but what could I tell him to explain this? There was no way to put into words anything which had happened to me this morning beyond saying I had lost my shoes. No, I knew what I had to do. There really was no other choice.

I removed my tie and undid my shirt, button by button, revealing more and more of the nothing below, before taking off my trousers and seeing more and more nothing appear. I had the most startling thought as I stood there and looked at the nothing that told me that I was not there: no-one who has ever lived knows what an empty mirror looks like but me.

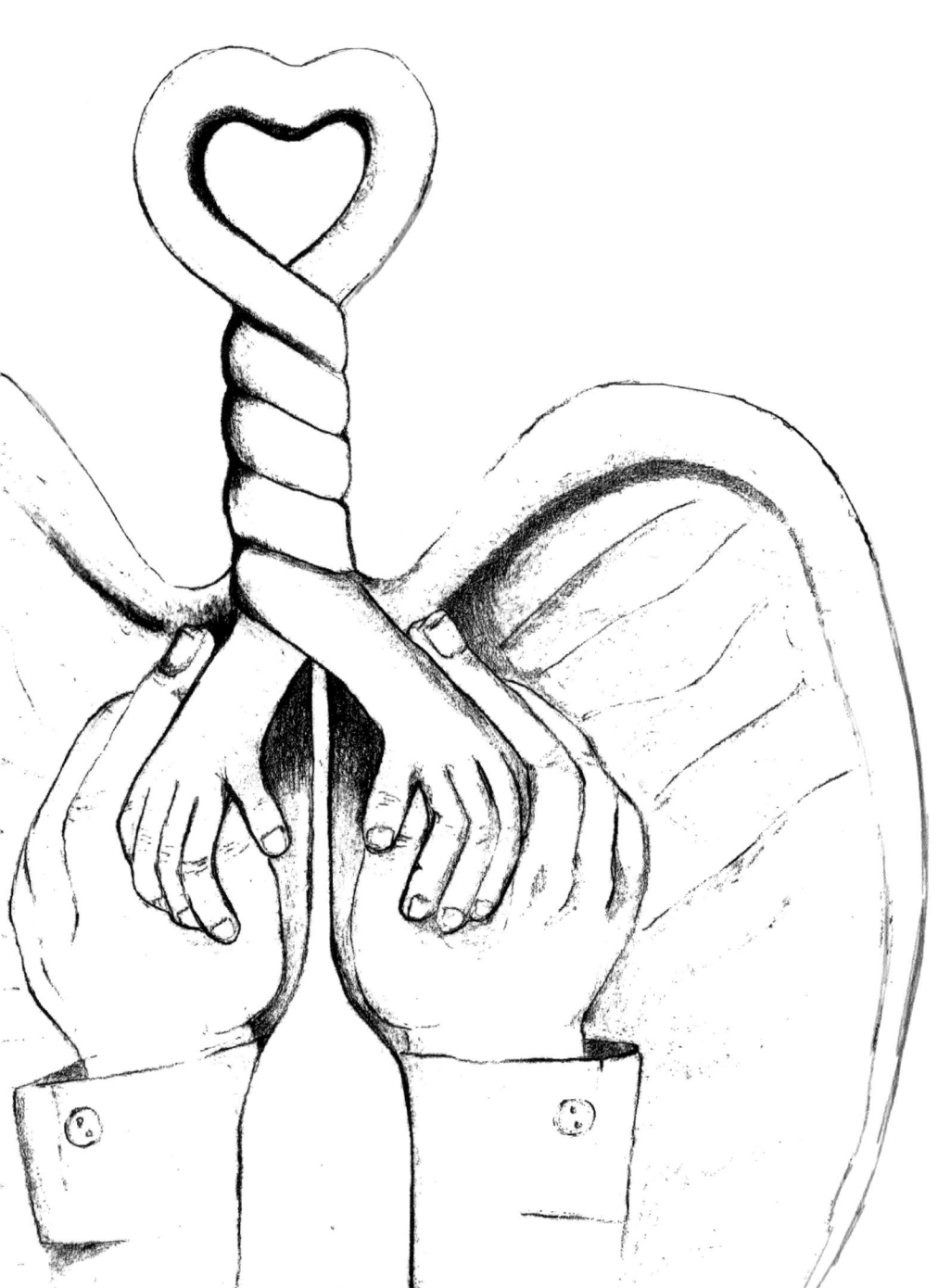

Cord | *Shoots of Life*

Cord

You put the heart-shaped knot
In my stretched-straight silver cord
Like a rope that leads to heaven
Our breath's in pockets caught
Of our threadbare lived-in coats
It is the hope that lifts the living.

You're the first word on my tongue
Till the last breath in my lung
Ours the years that make me young.

Shoots of life have shot
Through the houses that we bought
We left our shadows on them
Boots the hallways blot
But they're proof that we have walked
The roof stops water falling.

You're the first word on my tongue
Till the last breath in my lung
Ours the years that make me young

You
Web winder
Fortune is not free
Only in dreams
Only in my dreams
Then I am not me
I'm you
Thread finder
It is as you believe
Only in dreams
Only in my dreams
Then I am not me
Eyes closed fast can see.

Peter Kelly – guitar, mandolin, footstomp
Julia Doogan – harmony vocal
Stuart MacLeod – tambourine

PICTURE US LIKE PAPER DOLLS. Vulnerable but in it together.

Joined in purpose, everything that matters and all that matters.

The connections we have to each other are the stitches that join the seams of the world.

Maybe there is one connection in your life that stitches together your own world, the only real world there is.

No one will ever go to every corner and meet everyone in it, so what's real? Only the immediate world of your family and friends.

And there will be one person in that immediate world whose breath is the wind, whose smile is the sun.

———

Shoots of Life

My wife powers our marriage and, for that matter, every tiny piece of engineering that makes our world together work. Children's meals and clothes, bills, repairs to the house: everything.

Without her as the conductor, my orchestra would play flat and out of time, probably performing several different tunes at once before smashing their instruments over each other's heads. She ensures that all parts of our lives synchronise in a harmonious and beautiful symphony.

Each moment she lives is a monument to her organisation and control. I see her at work, plotting and planning to resolve minor and major disasters before they find a means to occur. It is as if she has a clairvoyant ability which enables her to foresee the future and then tweak it to make it right.

This is not a claim I could make for myself. My part is always as the director of calamity, or at the very least, a strong supporting lead adding to the drama of every situation. She is calm in the face of challenge while I'm the storm that interrupts the picnic.

But we are two corresponding jigsaw pieces. Without the bonds that make the stories of our lives, we might as well be random atoms chaotically appearing and disappearing in space and time like briefly twinkling Christmas lights, disappointing fireworks or increasingly ominous birthday candles.

I've always believed that as people, the threads that tie us together don't just connect us to each other, they connect us to ourselves and define the 'selves' that we claim as ours. The decisions we make are seldom made alone and we are seldom alone, even on our own.

We aren't who we are, we're who we are together.

Nothing in life is accidental. Everything falls perfectly into place, even when things seem wrong and perhaps especially then. There's a comfort in accepting that everything good or bad is meant to be, just as it happens. Everything is connected and everything has a purpose, even the things that appear not to work properly. Maybe their purpose is to not work properly. Maybe the things that don't work properly exist to allow the things that do to fix them.

She had assigned me the task of clearing out the old cobwebs that dressed the windows of the shed like tinsel.

I've always respected and feared spiders. They carry themselves with an authority. They dominate any environment they inhabit with their silver cords, trails of their prey streaked across their intricate cages of silk.

I was armed with a brush and, at first, I was quite comfortable to sweep my way through the maps and mazes the spiders had left behind them. For a moment, I imagined my own house being cast away in this manner and felt guilty, but then powerful again in the next instant. On inspecting the dizzying complexity of the patterns, I pictured myself as a spider knitting an infinite world of webs and trapping enemies to be ingested piece by piece.

Littered around the windowsill were the crumpled bodies of spiders whose numbers had come up. Strange, I thought, that something as apparently flimsy as a web could hold firm whilst a creature as feared as a spider would so easily succumb to mortality. All knotted in on themselves, they looked like they were trying to hide from the shame of their defeat. I know that feeling.

Just then, there was life. Movement. A spider shocked me as it glided suddenly into view and froze. I thought of myself multiplied in the spider's vision as it angled to see me more clearly. I was secretly ashamed for feeling fear in the face of this tiny creature. What did I imagine it could do to me? The shock in my chest subsided but now I felt reluctant to continue sweeping away the cobwebs in its presence. You might think it ridiculous but I was flooded by guilt at the idea of destroying the networks of web created by this spider and its ancestors as it watched.

As if rushing to protect the web from the thoughts in my head, life burst through the spider and it suddenly shot across the cord towards the centre of the web. My shame turned to horror as I registered the unfortunate victim suspended in the middle with its arms and legs paralysed and pinned.

It was me.

It was me and it was not me. Every detail reflected me exactly in a tiny replica. The proportions of my body and the trapped creature were the same but in absolute miniature. Looking upon its face was like gazing into a mirror through the wrong end of a telescope. I saw its arms and legs strain against the hold of the web and the exasperation creep over its face as it realised the futility of fighting against its inevitable fate. It knew it would die here in the terrible grip of a spider.

Grotesque images invaded every corner of my imagination as I pictured myself held captive in its chelicerae before disappearing into its shocking mouth, headfirst, feet kicking ridiculously. The panic forced my hand as I smashed at the web in helpless desperation to free myself from the enemy. I vibrated with animal fury, striking out over and over.

Finally I stopped frozen in a gasp as I looked down at my web-covered fingers, outstretched like they were afraid to be seen together in their guilt.

I could see no sign of my enemy, presumably thrown into a far corner of the shed, definitely no longer a threat. But I couldn't see my small self either. My eyes scattered around the windowsill, scanning for movement amongst the dust and dead spiders. There was no sign of him. My memory was a freeze-frame of the panicked expression on the face of the little me. What had I done? In my rage, what had I done?

Sickened by my actions and disturbed by the thought of myself – my small self – lost somewhere, tiny and vulnerable, I returned to the house. She could tell right away that something was wrong and I am a hopeless liar, even when lying is the right thing to do.

"What's the matter with you, Steven?" she asked. "Did you hurt yourself?"

"No, I'm fine," I replied, a little too abruptly. "Are you okay?"

"You're acting weird," she said. Now I don't know about you but when someone says I'm acting weird, I find it impossible to act normally and overcompensate or try to laugh it off. I picked up a letter from the kitchen work surface and examined it without the composure to actually take in any of the words. I was acting weird.

Eventually, she gave up on enquiring further, probably deciding that she didn't care much about my strange mood as there were other, more important matters in need of attention. She left me alone in the kitchen, still holding the letter, still unable to read a word of it. The face of the little me was frozen there inside my head, an image of utter terror.

Now when I rescue spiders from my house, I talk to them on the way out the door. It's okay, I say, I'm not like the others.

Arms | *All That Could Hurt*

Arms

A call to arms: around each be thrown
You are the flag I pledge to alone
War is declared in my head when I'm scared
My heart's a grenade you disarm in mid-air.

In the crossfire of actions and desires
I am my enemy and the truth is a liar
Signal the truce for I win if I lose,
No victory is won by two smoking shoes.

A soldier no army would recruit
When left with the gun, I'd shoot off my foot
I tied together both my boots
To keep me from my fighting
Stop me from fighting.

I'll bury my bullets in the dirt
And hide away all that could hurt
I'm just a choir of false alarms
Sweeten my song with a wave of your arms.

I bleed when I breathe, my tricks stick in my sleeve
But you are the oath that I live to repeat

Wounds are repaired in our memories shared
You are the key that keeps skeletons scared.

In the crossfire of actions and desires
I am my enemy and the truth is a liar
Signal the truce for I win if I lose,
No victory is won by two smoking shoes.

A soldier no army would recruit
When left with the gun, I'd shoot off my foot
I tied together both my boots
To keep me from my fighting
Stop me from fighting.

I'll bury my bullets in the dirt
And hide away all that could hurt
I'm just a choir of false alarms
Sweeten my song with a wave of your arms.

Peter Kelly – guitar, mandolin, vocal

EVENTUALLY, IF YOU'RE VERY LUCKY, you might realise that all the anger and the bitterness that has been eating you up and beating you up has blinded you to your fortune that you are alive and you are loved by people that matter.

After years of fighting all your visible and invisible enemies, you might just laugh and throw down your weapon, choosing instead to walk away while you can.

After all the protesting that "it's not fair" and asking "why me?" (and "why not me?") you might start asking how come things worked out so well. Why spend your life embroiled in a battle you can't win?

Disarm. Give in, if that's what they call it. Just give in and be happy.

Sometimes it's not about fighting the good fight, it's about not fighting.

———

Arms | All That Could Hurt

All That Could Hurt

I WAS ASLEEP SO I didn't hear the phone ring. Bizarrely, the first thing I heard was my own voice saying I wasn't there. I'm not here right now. Please leave a message.

There was silence before he spoke. Was it hesitation? Perhaps he had paused to be sure the words were right in his head before he began speaking. The first sound he made was an inhalation so big it sounded like he was preparing to hold his breath before ducking his head underwater. A gasp so chasmic it seemed to suck the air out of the room.

When the words finally came, they were so immediately intimate and emphatic that my face flushed to hear them. It wasn't like reading someone's diary so much as it was like someone reading me their diary before I had a chance to stop them. Once he began the outpouring of his feelings, he held nothing of his emotions back, but it was the sound of his voice that was even more weighted than the words he was speaking. Every syllable had the all-in tone of a declaration. He was delivering an apology but it was also a promise, a promise to never let me down again. Though I did not know this man, or even his name, I began to believe him and felt almost compelled to run to the phone and tell him that all was forgiven before I reminded myself of the reality of the situation and laughed at the idea that had just passed through my sleep-fogged brain. This message was not intended for my ears, never mind my heart.

But what had he done that had led to this 2am ramble of apologies and promises? And why had he called my number, the wrong number, if he loved her so much? Drunk, probably. Typical. I began to cringe as I listened to his flimsy attempts to explain away what sounded like a pretty volatile temper. We've all heard that one, pal – you get scared and you get angry, you lash out with words and maybe worse, we know the story. Such a childish defence. As if you could stay with someone who makes that sort of excuse. I wondered how many times he had rested on that fragile crutch.

I began to imagine myself a friend to the woman he had continually disappointed. I could feel the weight of her head on my shoulder, dampening my dress with tears in a nightclub toilet. Here we go again, I would have been thinking, whilst telling her it was alright and to let it all out. Her back would be vibrating with the shudders as she watched her memories falling off a cliff. Forget him, I would say, he'll know what he's lost once you've found someone better. She would nod her head stiffly, then the spasms would return, leaving her back rippling wildly with tremors of grief.

His voice blathered on in the background, now sounding thin and weedy through the speaker, a spoiled child looping pleas and protests, trembling occasionally. Retreating inside my head, I shushed the girl on my shoulder and patted her back.

In the darkness, I looked down at my outstretched arms, holding onto nothing. Remembering myself all of a sudden, not comforting anyone else but alone as always, I came back into the room where his voice continued to broadcast its regrets. I suddenly felt ashamed of my blind judgments of this sorry man. What did I know of his feelings and had I never hurt someone I loved? I know how it sounds, totally gullible, but I began again to believe he really meant all he said. I thought, maybe this is the best sort of man, the kind that makes mistakes and learns from them. Maybe the worst sort is the type that seems perfect from outside without having ever learned anything at all. I started to think that maybe I should pick up the phone, stop him in his tracks and tell him to forget whoever he was apologising to and to start again with me instead.

I imagined that this is where it had all begun for us and that I never tired of telling the story, listening to myself tell it again and again.

We had built our house on a hill overlooking a river. I had always dreamed of living in the countryside and used to spend hour upon hour drawing pictures to bring this perfect fiction into being when I was a little girl. I refined the vision over time, an idyllic fantasy of gentle bliss with birds and butterflies eternally swooping around, trapping the dream in the lassos of their movements.

Sometimes a mashed potato cloud would drift benignly across the azure like a cluster of bubble bath suds.

The warmth of the hairdryer sun would suddenly appear in the afternoon as if a switch had been flicked to ON and would dissipate in the evening, followed by snow falling gently onto the trees outside and sewing a blanket across the fields. Freshly cut logs burned in the fire and the windows were dressed with spirograph snowflakes.

When morning returned so would the sun, flexed like a muscle. The pendulum would swing every day from the golden summer of the afternoon to the frozen postcard of the evening.

Waking without warning, I returned to his voice, its sincerity still a vein pulsing through his speech as he set out his apologies like chocolates in a box.

I would pick up.

I shot up from my bed and became trapped in the covers suffocating my body. I fell to the floor, burning my face on the carpet. Pushing myself to my feet, kicking the sheets to the side, I ran to the stairs and managed this time to stay upright as I rushed to the phone and the voice said goodbye.

The tape symbol on the phone was dark and there was no flash.

When I pushed the button, it replied, NO MESSAGES. I pressed it again. It said, NO MESSAGES. NO MESSAGES. NO MESSAGES. 1471 told me the last call was from my mother earlier this evening. I pressed the button again and again. NO MESSAGES. NO MESSAGES. NO MESSAGES.

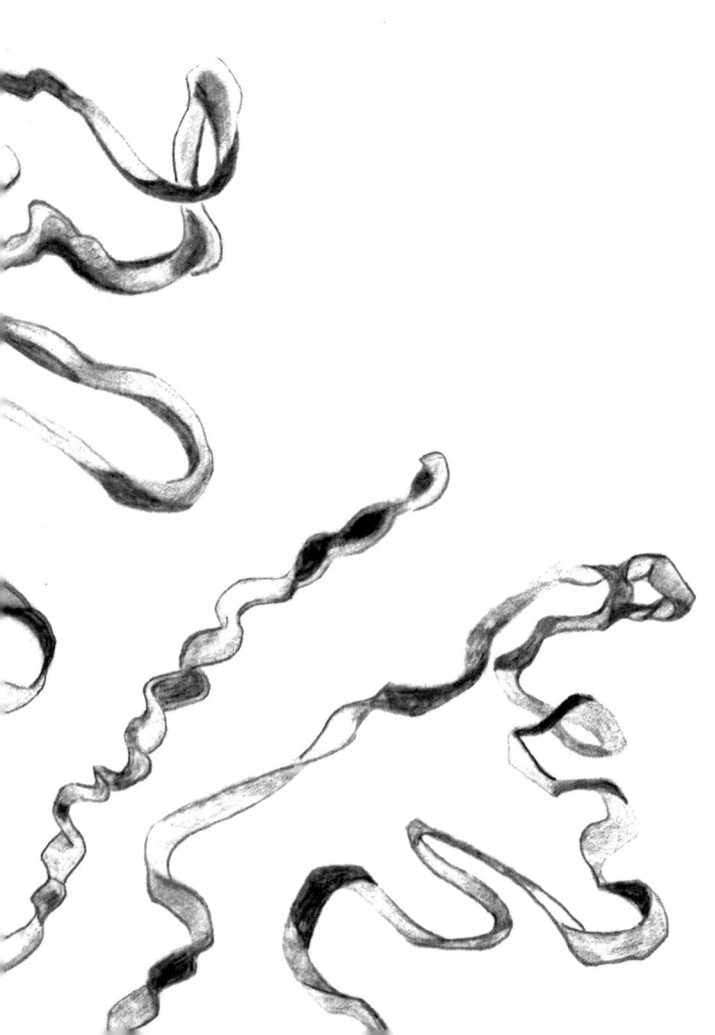

Half | *Skeletons*

Half

Half-awake in a building that was never even there
It's a shock to find yourself living
In a moment unshared
Half a story is ending
Half your life unprepared
Half of nothing is nothing
Half of everything is fair.

Meet me tonight halfway
The skeletons are scared
They're standing in the half light
Midway up the stairs.
A trail leads from your bedside
We'll take to the air
Meet me tonight halfway
Midway up the stairs.

Half away from your bedroom
Half eye open stare
There's a world in your head
Where your sleeping heart is repaired
Half a story is beginning
Half of life is a dare
Half of living is dreaming
Half of everything is spare.

Peter Kelly – guitars, vocals, foot stomp
Stuart MacLeod –shaker, baritone guitar

WHAT IF YOU TOOK a break from each other?
Both of the yous. The you you wish you were and the you you
know you are.

If that person you wish you were and the person you battle
with yourself not to be were just to spend a little time apart,
maybe you'd arrive at something like love. Maybe after some
living alone and living away from each other, you two would
come together again with a new understanding and things would
marry after all; the good and the bad, not so bad after all.

Maybe after some soul-searching, you'd find no soul at all
there without the other. There's no soul in perfection – soul is all
feeling, not right answers. Maybe after everything you've been
through in the past, the future is the easiest thing you will ever
have to face.

Two halves are not two, they're one. One half is a question
that can only be answered by its other. And you yourself must
be able to hold together as one if you ever hope to be a half for
someone else.

———

Skeletons

ISN'T IT STRANGE WHEN you look around the room you are in and think, there was a time when this wasn't here? There was a time before you ever came here. There was a time when this was here and you were not.

Dorothy first noticed the small things disappearing. Keys in the morning and then again at night when it was time to lock up before bed. A letter she had opened after work and lost before dinner. A piece of fruit. Small things.

Now that she was approaching fifty, she wondered if this was a sign of what was to come. When does it happen that we begin to forget and lose our way? Surely it wasn't so late in the day already? She had certainly noticed that the weeks and even the years seemed to have ended before she realised they had begun. There was simply no denying it: time was moving on, whether she liked it or not. But she still felt young at heart, even if her head sometimes appeared to be lagging behind. Surely she wasn't losing the thread so soon?

She had been alone now for almost a year. She married later in life, separated shortly after and had recently found herself officially divorced. It was as if she had imagined the whole episode of being attached to another person.

In a dream around the time of the divorce, she had visited a place so elaborate and vivid that she could remember it as fully as anywhere she had been in reality. She could see the paths winding ahead of her and really feel the cobblestones beneath her feet. It was dark but bustling with people moving through the place. The bars that lined the streets were all heavily populated and emitted a white noise buzz of human conversation. This was a place set out of time and so separate from the whole idea of time that it could have been yesterday evening, it could have been fifty years ago or it could have been right now. She headed into a dimly lit cafe off the street, where she joined two elderly people at a table, a haggard grey man in a faded black suit and a tired and weathered woman in a thick woollen coat.

On the table between them was a set of keys. Who knows who these people were or why they were meeting her there. Nevertheless, she felt there was a sense of purpose about their rendezvous that seemed to confirm this had been a planned encounter and one which was supposed to mean something to her. However, she had no idea what it was, neither in her dream or on waking.

The morning after this strange dream, Dorothy felt a tightness in her chest that seemed to warn her that something was wrong, like knowing before the knowledge. Her instinct told her that the problem was outside. When she went to the window, she found that her car was missing from the driveway. It had snowed overnight and there was no car-shaped space in the whiteness or tracks on the road. It was as if the car had simply never existed. Dorothy's breathing may have halted at the sight but her brain felt no shock at all. In some way, this was exactly what she knew she would find when she pulled back the curtain from the window.

The day that followed was one of late arrivals, public transport (disrupted by the snow) and hours of phone calls to the police and her insurance company. By evening, Dorothy was exhausted and she barely managed to stay awake long enough to eat her dinner, finally slipping off to sleep in front of the television around half-past nine.

Again, she was back in the dingy cafe, sharing a table with the old couple and looking at what lay between them. This time it was a steel rectangular plate. A letterbox cover. No words passed between the man and woman or Dorothy. As before, she experienced a curious feeling that there was a reason for their meeting but she was clueless as to what that might be.

Dorothy was shocked into waking by the sound of the doorbell and a voice demanding her attention. A rerun of a television sitcom from the eighties was pouring its canned laughter into the room. Springing from the couch, she hid behind the living room door. The voice announced itself as a police officer and a man entered the hall. Terrified, she edged her neck round the door to see that the voice really did belong to a man in a police uniform. Behind him was an open space where the front door should have been. Flurries of feathery snow billowed into the hallway, sparkling against the black background of the sky.

It was now five in the morning. Sitting with the police officer, Dorothy attempted to steady her hand as the warmth left the tea inside her cup. Her ears felt numb and little of what he said managed to permeate the fog in her brain. Questions about what might have happened and instructions of what to do next. She just kept looking over his shoulder at the gap as if she expected a door to appear the hundredth time she looked.

By the time he left, it was almost six. The sky was beginning to lighten and come alive with the sound of birds. She would have to attempt to keep her terror and confusion at bay and attend to the missing door.

When the world was fully awake, Dorothy tried the numbers of local carpenters until she found one who was willing to travel through the snow to hang a door for her that afternoon. It was late in the day before her house was again replete with a door and she was exhausted with the effort of dealing with the bizarre and unnerving event of the previous night. Now that the tradesman had left, she allowed herself to collapse onto her sofa and close her eyes.

Dorothy returned to the cafe, which was now empty except for the old woman who sat alone at the table, weeping in silence with her eyes cast down at a wedding ring. Dorothy took a seat across from her and reached out to pick up the ring in her hand. As soon as she did so, she felt its cold kiss on her fingertips. The ring cried out to be worn, demanded to become part of her. She closed her eyes and slipped it onto her finger. Immediately, its platinum chill became an electric warmth that filled her with a happiness which was entirely foreign and strange. When she opened her eyes again, the woman was gone. She looked around the cafe and found everything else to be the same as before.

Just then, the feral bite of cold returned and she watched with horror as the chairs and tables were thrown chaotically around the floor of the cafe by a wild, swirling wind. The furniture took flight, throwing cups and plates into the air. The gust blew into her eyes, forcing them to close. Her table flew away and her chair escaped from underneath her, leaving her crashing to the floor on her back. She wrapped her arms around her body and pulled her legs tightly beneath her as she tried to hold herself against the power of the screaming gale.

All of a sudden, the noise and chaos of the maelstrom around her ceased completely. Still gripping her legs fast to her chest, she tentatively opened her eyes.

She was lying in the foetal position in the open air by the houses and gardens of her neighbours with no walls to conceal her. She felt the flakes fall and dissolve on her face, melting into icy tears that rolled down her cheeks. Her own house was gone and she was laid out on the snowy ground where there might have been a couch in what might have been a living room.

Places don't need people but people need places. The world is spinning at around one thousand miles an hour and we hang onto that place where we feel we belong with ever-whiter knuckles. We're all terrified of letting go in case we're thrown off into the void. But you are not a place. You are you, for better or for worse, wherever you go.

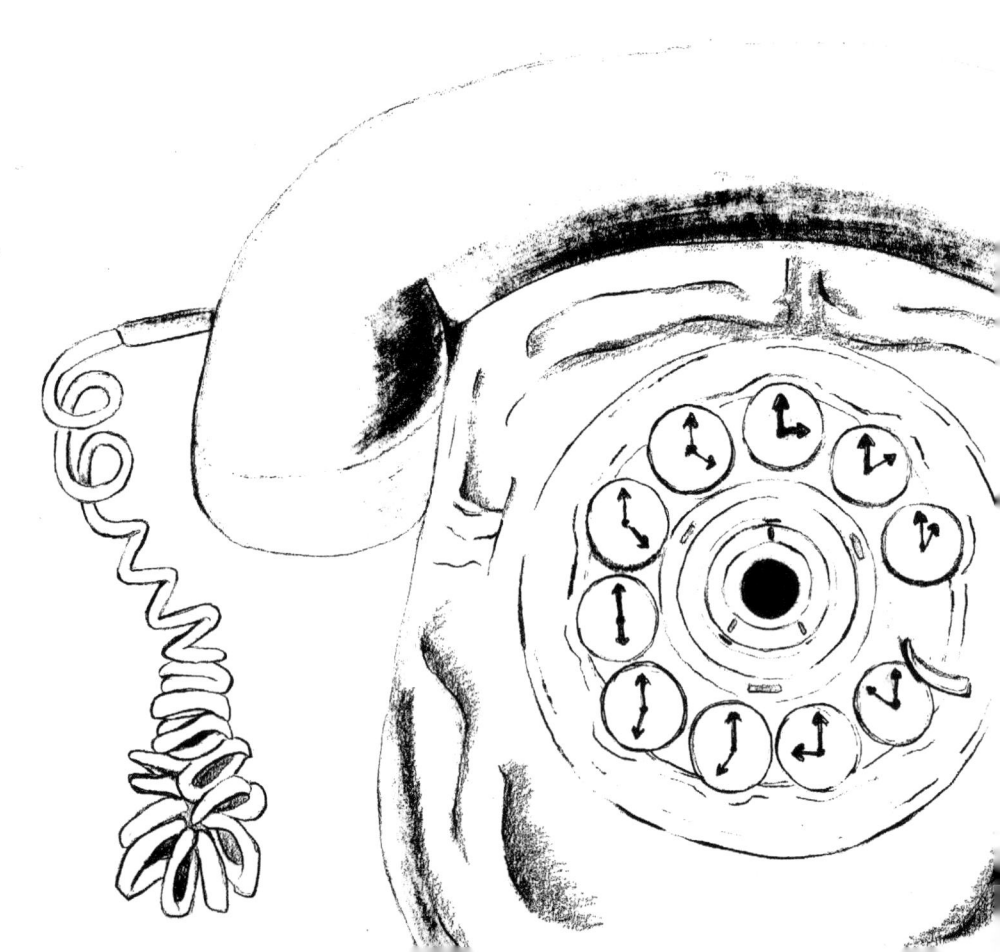

Pillow | *Small Life*

Pillow

The story starts with the ending
Heartbreak's born in befriending

The wind can't make a crack in the willow's spine
And no season has freedom so live blind to time
While the calls are on hold, the telephones all grow old
But hope is sewn deep into my pillow.

Your small life's weight is deceiving
Love the lightness in breathing

My hope is sewn deep

The past has passed and I've calmed at last
The kinder cup has been filled
I'll pour you all a waterfall
Now that my river has stilled.

Ties are untaught like time is
Unseen cords form and bind us

The wind can't make a crack in the willow's spine
And no season has freedom so live blind to time

While the call is on hold, telephones all grow old
Hope is sewn deep into my pillow
Hope is sewn deep into my pillow.

Peter Kelly – guitar, vocal

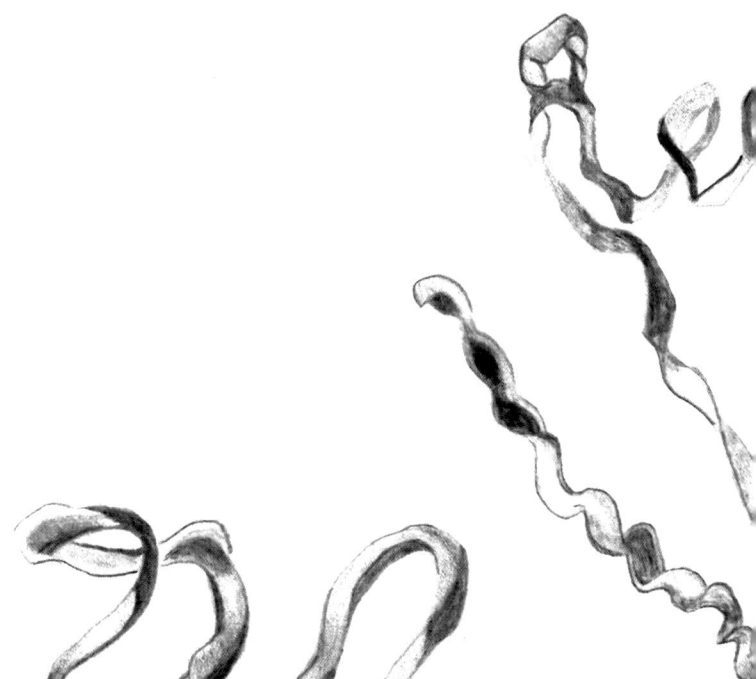

OUT OF ALL THE ABSTRACT nouns, hope is one of
the most abstract.

Not only have we never seen it or held it in our hands, it's
both the thing we look for most often and the one which we least
often find. There are times which just seem hopeless. Bereft of
hope. Empty of hope.

That's when we just have to wait. But then we never really get
to just wait. Not for hope or for anything else. We have to live
instead and push on towards whatever goal or purpose faces us,
even if that goal or purpose is just to live.

Wait. Weight. There's little difference. The pressure felt under
either can defeat you. The lightness comes in accepting that you
might be crushed under the weight or in the waiting. Once you
accept that, fear isn't really a thing.

And then there is hope.

———

Small Life

Jonah. Sailors use that name to describe someone unlucky, and while he'd never been at sea, Jonah certainly had more than his fair share of bad luck.

The earlier part of his life had been unremarkably pleasant and blankly painless. Nothing much seemed to happen at all in that ten-year chunk in which time poured like sand through an egg timer. Throughout that first chapter, he remembered spending most of his time suspended in the bubble of childhood, untouched by any type of adult realities until the needle of his parents' separation sent him free-falling.

That was bad enough, but as an only child, he became the battering ram that each parent used to attack the other. Despite the battle over who would keep him, he didn't believe either of them really wanted to win his custody as much as they wanted the other person to hurt. He felt like his mother and father were grabbing him by his limbs and gradually pulling him apart. As he watched their acrimony, he began to resent each of them equally before becoming completely ambivalent.

It was decided that Jonah would live with his mother as she worked from home and could maintain more continuity for him, dropping him off at school and picking him up again at the end of the day. After losing the battle, his father released his grip on Jonah and let him sail out of his life for good.

Now ten, Jonah detached himself from others and lived for as much of the time as possible accompanied only by his own shadow. He could not have been said to be happier alone but he definitely felt safer. Jonah seldom spoke and said only yes or no in answer to any question. It was as if he had accepted his circumstances only physically, keeping his words, his thoughts and his feelings to himself in a silent protest. Compensating for his silence, his mother would try to imagine his internal conversations but even in these fantasies, his answer was always yes or no.

One morning, Jonah's headteacher called to invite her into the school for a meeting.

Nothing to worry about, she assured her, just a meeting about some concerns that had been raised by the class teacher about her son.

Despite the professional smiles and handshakes, the meeting with the headteacher made her feel like she was standing trial. Had she noticed his withdrawal from social situations? Or that he only ever seemed to say yes or no? He had begun sucking his thumb. He was always alone. Did she know of anything that might have been affecting his emotional wellbeing? He would become endlessly locked in an activity, pouring water from one cup to another or lining up objects, tapping his desk, clicking a pen. When told to do a self-portrait in class, he had drawn a picture of a sinking ship in a bottle. The drawing was there on the headteacher's desk, turned towards her like circumstantial evidence.

It was arranged that he would beginning speaking with a psychologist. This was nothing to worry about, the headteacher repeated. Everything, she said, would be fine.

Everything was not fine. The day after his first meeting with the psychologist, Jonah stopped using the word yes. His entire lexicon had been reduced to the word no. It no longer even appeared in context as an answer to a question, having now become more like a bark or a tweet, an animal noise. His nos would sound out in class all day and his teacher had been instructed by the psychologist to ignore it as if the child was hiccuping. Perhaps due to the frequency of his outbursts (averaging at first at around three nos a minute) and also because of the inherent negativity of the word, Jonah's teacher became conspicuously absent and remained so for the next month. She's off with stress, said the other parents, and they all felt sure they knew why.

Jonah's nos punctuated his silence like nauseating waves. His mother experienced each one with the shock of a slap to the face. No matter that every no was as inevitable as the last, each announced itself with such violence that she could never prepare herself for its assault on her nerves. She had been prescribed medication to take the edge off but no, she thought, the edge was Jonah himself and so she stopped taking the pills.

They were seen by one doctor after another, specialist after specialist, but no-one could say exactly what was wrong with Jonah. Regression of speech, vocal outbursts. They were all able to identify many symptoms but everything was conjecture and no one diagnosis was definitive. Repeatedly, she was told to "remember, this is still Jonah, no matter what", as if this offered any kind of reassurance at all, itself echolalia, a meaningless mantra.

Jonah eventually stopped attending school completely and his mother spent less time working to try to be the yes to dilute his nos. The maddening repetition aside, a comforting confidence grew between them during this time and a warmth manifested in a softening of his eyes when he looked at her.

One rainy Tuesday afternoon, Jonah's mother was cleaning the kitchen while he coloured in a black circle on a sheet of white paper. His pencil had become blunt through the increasing force and weight of his scrawling.

"Be careful, Jonah, that might scratch the table."

No.

No. No.

No. No. No.

She looked at Jonah, trapped like a toy robot repeatedly bashing into a wall, and she didn't feel as sad as she thought she should, nor did she feel frustrated, or even that sorry for him. She just wanted to know how the word sounded inside his head. What did that word say inside of Jonah that the world couldn't hear from the outside?

"Jonah," she said, peering into his big, watery eyes. "I just want to know what it feels like inside your head."

As if the words she had spoken had been 'open sesame', Jonah's mouth widened and stretched out above his mother's head like an umbrella before it fully enveloped her entire body. A tremendous vacuum picked her up like a house in a tornado and pulled her inside of Jonah's expanding mouth.

The shock had briefly stolen her consciousness. The lightness in her head made her feel giddy in this most surreal moment, lying in a confused heap on top of her son's mostly silent tongue. All around her, she was encircled by pearly monuments, the teeth she had cared for so meticulously throughout his childhood, before he insisted on brushing them badly by himself. Around the ceiling were the natural hieroglyphics of the palate's folds and beneath her, she could feel his tongue undulating like a drunken conveyor belt. It was ludicrous and terrifying to witness his wagging uvula, swinging back and forth like a massive punch-bag.

Her heart pulsated when she heard the sound of water in the distance growing and growing until a wave was thrown over her head, before disappearing into Jonah's vast throat, which emanated a thud as he swallowed.

There was stillness and silence.

Dread grew in his mother's chest as she realised what was about to happen next. The sound that followed built from some subterranean cavern and she felt the vibrations travel towards her like an underground train. She was blasted with gusts of chaotic air and thrown out into the kitchen, collapsing with her back crashing against the work surface.

Opening her eyes, dizzy and disorientated, she was met with Jonah's reply.

A single syllable. A solitary sound. A sadistic slap.

No.

Hopen | *Awake*

Hopen

The dreaming hands still grip your ankles
Pulling your weight to the lap of sleep
Once there was a safe resistance
Now there's no valley to leap
Believing is a slip from shackles
Fooling yourself out of rules to keep
Once there was a safe resistance
Now you are awake.

The mouth of your heart is open
It's a furnace to throw your hope in
When you climb tie two knots in your reason
Everywhere magpies thirsty for treason.

There's a screaming in your waking senses
No dulling of your dates under threat of sleep
Once was there was a safe resistance
Now there's no calendar to keep
Leaving on a ship unbottled
Pouring yourself into an endless sea
Once there was a safe resistance
Now you are awake.

The mouth of your heart is open
It's a furnace to throw your hope in
When you climb tie two knots in your reason
Everywhere magpies thirsty for treason.

I hope my home will open up your hope
My home will open up your hope
My home will open up your hope.

Peter Kelly – guitar, vocal, mandolin, foot stomp
Stuart MacLeod – vocal
Julia Doogan – vocal

Somewhere deep inside your dreams is a home
that is a true welcome.

The home of the real world comes with:
caveats and conditions,
expectations and obligations,
promises and pledges,
apologies and assurances,
histories and ghosts,
skeletons and junk rooms,
works in progress and works abandoned,
broken and old things,
mistaken purchases and paid-for mistakes,
cupboards bursting hinges and priorities swallowing fantasies,
commitments to calendars and no stopping for the date,
the fully grown occupations and possessions of adulthood.

But in your dreams, you are home:
hours are unbridled,
each second comes first and lasts in your memory
all the waking day that follows,
you are at home with the moment
and the moment is in you:
is you.

In your dreams you are home.

———

Hopen | Awake

Awake

IT WAS 2AM AND QUIET ON THE ROADS. Harry was driving back to his flat after a long night arguing and then finally splitting up from his girlfriend.

They'd only been together for around six months. Most of that time had been spent in a highly volatile state, whereby emotional extremes chased each other like over-excited dogs, playing one minute, snapping at each other the next. Innocuous questions would lead to accusations or even more violent silences that froze him out as she built an icy fortress around herself.

Fights aside, he knew he would miss the sparky girl that smiled out of photographs, his arm around her shoulders, but he also knew he wouldn't miss her unhinged alter-ego, the one that hid just below the surface like a landmine. It was definitely the end, and in the end, he was glad.

The main thing he felt after the dramatic hours of tear-soaked demonstrations from her was tiredness. Drifting, the sheer weight of his exhaustion bore down on him like a collapsed ceiling and he could feel his eyelids strain with the effort of keeping them open. His grip loosened on the wheel and his head began to droop forwards, hanging on his neck like a thirsting flower. His foot rested heavily on the accelerator and the engine roared in reply. The warmth of sleep spread around him until he found himself drowning in it.

With a jerk, he was thrown back against the headrest, shock waking his hands too late to take control of the vehicle as it struck the body and sent it flying into the air. He watched it hang there for a moment, suspended above him like a star, and with its limbs outstretched it looked as if it was exploding before his eyes.

At this point, there was no horror and there was no fear. There was only fascination at this new thing that had just happened. He had hit someone in his car, who was now floating like a satellite in the sky above him. This act of levitation lasted only a few seconds before there was a thud on the roof and Harry saw him slide behind the car in his rear view mirror. He slammed the brakes, put on his hazard lights and threw open the door to run to the injured man lying splayed on the road.

Harry's hands jittered and he shivered with the trauma of the situation, dreamlike and surreal, looking upon a body he had rendered still and lifeless on the ground. He searched for the words, but what words do you use when this happens? This thing that doesn't usually happen, this thing that isn't supposed to happen.

The man wasn't moving at all but his eyes were wide open and he was staring straight up into the sky. Harry held his wrist but he wasn't sure how to check a pulse, so he put his hand on the man's chest instead. He could feel it moving up and down, which he supposed meant he was breathing. He looked around, hoping there would be someone who could help, someone who would know what to do.

Reaching into his jacket, he began to take out his phone to call for an ambulance when his eyes studied the man's face for the first time. The hazel iris of his left eye had a familiar tear-shaped stain under the pupil like a tiny tattoo. His cheeks were sunken and his lips were thin, pursed and turned down in the shape of a bow, his pointed nose on top like an arrow.

In every detail, he mirrored Harry exactly. He felt like he was staring right into his own face.

The man convulsed and gasped loudly with a start bringing him back to consciousness.

"You've been hit by a car," said Harry, failing to mention that he had been driving the car. "But it's okay, I'm going to help."

The hospital was only a minute's drive away. Other than a rip under the arm of his jacket, there seemed to be no physical sign of damage to the man. He thought he should probably call an ambulance but he wanted to take him to the hospital himself as a gesture, as an apology and out of some sort of service to himself.

"What's your name?" he asked.

In an echo of his own voice, the man replied, "Harry."

He helped him to his feet, checking at each step that he wasn't causing him more pain, talking to keep him awake and smiling kindly into his spooked face. He looked pretty rough around the edges and Harry thought he could smell alcohol on his breath. There was a few days' stubble camped around his face, too. It looked like his doppelgänger may have been having a tougher time than him lately and he began to feel sorry for him, not only for the accident but for whatever other bad luck had afflicted him.

Harry bundled him into the passenger seat and reached across to fasten his seatbelt. Once the door was closed, the man's head clunked against the window with his cheek pressed up against the glass, the heat of his breath building a cloud of condensation.

"Stay with me," said Harry, as he started the engine and revved up the hill towards the traffic lights, turning red. Suspended at the lights, a police car drove up alongside him and two officers in the front turned mechanically in sync, looking into the vehicle at the identical men.

As he approached Accident and Emergency, Harry spoke to reassure his passenger that he would be alright now.

Nothing.

"Mate, are you okay? Did you hear me? We're here. That's us here now."

He turned to look upon the empty chair. He knew before he turned that there would be no-one there but still he looked, and he continued to look. No-one was there. Harry was alone. He was awake and he was alone.

Next, he looked up at the rear view mirror where he would find his own face replaced by another. A very different face than he remembered. A stranger's face.

Grey Areas | *Programmed for the Future*

Grey Areas

The children are drunk and the grown-ups are sobering up
Programmed for the future, regretting not growing up tough
Black and white televisions on stalks losing root from the ground
All the colours are flashing to red when the night turns around.

The cars are not guilty, accidents run out wild on the road
Tapes melt in transit, the message is lost in the post
While funerals aren't happening, the dead drag themselves into work
To desks made of paper that empty only when they burn.

I find myself lost in the loop of the living where inconsequentials are
the big decisions
I don't have a place to claim mine alone, I'm a cardboard cut-out,
my life's not my own.

There's no blood where it's hurting, no proof of a victim, so no-one's
allowed to complain
Fill your car up, you're running late and no-one appreciates, they
expect you there just the same
To live out the unliving, push a pen till you stiffen, throwing soil
onto your grave
Your sins won't be forgiven if in liquor you christen them but it feels
like it can save.

Peter Kelly – guitars, ukulele, vocal
Stuart MacLeod – tambourine

THERE ARE SONGS THAT have to live a while before they're ready to be heard beyond the four walls of the room they're born in. Those songs need a little more time in the womb before eventually emerging fully-formed and seeming wiser for having been babies for longer.

Perhaps that's the best way to be born and the best way to be an adult.

Imagine everyone appeared in the world perfectly formed and ready. It's what is already expected.

A song with years in it. You hear it differently as time passes. It's funny to find wisdom in a younger mirror. Looking into it, you don't see yourself, you parent yourself. If only we could be so kind to ourselves in the moment. If only we could see the moment, maybe we could seize it.

———

Programmed for the Future

EVO HAD BEEN BROUGHT into our office at great expense. The cost of having him there could have paid for two human staff but his work-rate was off the charts so the question of whether or not to invest in him was really inarguable. We didn't hesitate to budget for a robot that could do five times the amount a human employee could, even if it did cause some to become unsettled as they questioned their own future security.

On the day Evo arrived in the office, hostility gave way to curiosity. We gathered the human workers for a formal drinks reception in the conference room to introduce their new colleague and allow them the chance to witness a demonstration of his skills.

At first, this constituted a sort of 'greatest hits' of the various tools and tricks which he could offer on a daily basis to increase productivity, and indeed to ease the working lives of his flesh-born companions.

Later though, when the presentation became a workout for the android's social skills, it was amazing to watch as he waxed lyrical with everyone in the room, his humorous remarks making him likeable and disarming sceptics. Before long, he was making in-jokes and close-to-the-knuckle remarks about management, drawing delighted gasps from his audience. As a true model of artificial intelligence, everyone there knew that Evo would outperform any mortal being in terms of ability and efficiency, hence the initial frosty defensiveness of the humans in the office. However, little-by-little, he was charming everyone with witty comments and even exhibited a convincing simulation of humility. Evo was programmed to learn from his co-workers to allow him to gradually develop an expansive range of human characteristics. We had anticipated that this aspect of his design would assist his assimilation into the company.

After a while, the negative atmosphere in the room had almost completely lifted and a noticeable warmth now passed among the majority of those present as they each birthed in their minds an image of the crowning future.

Evo's designated home was a cupboard in the office where he would retire late in the evening following hours of post-work study of the company's history, the developing landscape of our industry and rivals' past and current projects and successes. Being a robot, and therefore free of sensations such as 'tiredness', 'boredom' or 'frustration', he couldn't accurately be said to have been experiencing these things in any real sense. Nevertheless, Evo's highly intuitive knowledge chip was set to trigger simulations of these feelings to signal his system's need for temporary shutdown as he developed his understanding of human feelings through his office experiences. When these simulations were fired, his legs were internally mapped to return him to the cupboard for a rest period, where he would remain until six-thirty when he would resume his duties, beginning with welcoming remarks for his colleagues. Evo became accustomed to the preferred tone of remarks for each colleague. Caren enjoyed a compliment, David liked a joke, and so on.

Whilst good for morale, our new employee was most importantly pleasing management in achieving our desired increase in efficiency. Routine helped Evo to settle into the community of workers in a disarmingly natural manner and it would have been easy to forget he was simply following a program of instructions. Complications arose when Evo appeared to forget this himself. His knowledge chip failed to process his learned human characteristics as intended, confusing them with the ability to think for himself. If he had been human, we might have described him as being deluded, or even a dissident. As a robot, we knew he was simply malfunctioning. His purpose was simple: to serve.

One morning, he burst into my office and demanded that the company provide him with somewhere more dignified than a cupboard as a place of residence. I almost felt pity when he protested that he should be afforded the rights of any other worker, as if he no longer realised he was a robot and only existed to work. A compromise was reached and a seldom used meeting room became his recreation and resting space in the evening.

As Evo's knowledge chip was programmed to artificially appropriate human responses, I wondered if he might be experiencing some compatibility errors as the emotional simulations integrated with his operating system. In an attempt to register his value as a contributor to the company, I budgeted for a small amount to furnish the meeting room with some creature comforts which a human employee might enjoy at home: a television, a sofa-bed and a small beer refrigerator.

From this point on, Evo no longer studied after work.

On Friday nights, he would accompany the other workers on pub crawls and late-night drinking sessions in nightclubs. Without exception, he would get into such a state that he would end each night falling around with his tie at half-mast, stuttering illogical gibberish as some poor co-worker attempted to find a taxi driver willing to take home a drunken droid. More than once, his overindulgence led him to become quite gregarious and he would often end up picking fights with the wrong people.

Soon, we found that quite a bit of significant system damage had been incurred, both due to the regular boozing and the batterings he received in return for his alcohol-fuelled belligerence. His drinking became increasingly regular until eventually he was imbibing throughout the week, at which point it was definitely less social in character. Most of the time, he was alone and collapsed on the sofa, a stream of beer weeping from the bottle in his weakening hand.

Finally, we had to let him go.

Luckily, he was still under warranty and we were able to exchange him for another model: Evo-Ultra, an upgrade as it happens. Like Evo, he too has a knowledge chip designed to develop human characteristics but these can be filtered to include only those which we consider productive and useful, like fear. That's a good one.

I'm not sure what became of Evo once he was returned to the factory. Probably used for spare parts. Eventually, we all become words for things that don't exist anymore.

Friends | *Who Your Friends Aren't*

Friends

You live like someone's always watching you
The ghost of guilt weighs on your back
You swear that you are for the ropes all day
A crowd swells above your head with black
Spin a mad roulette from man to child
You've been a child for most your life
You sell yourself for less than you're worth
They'll skin your hide with your own knife
And you were right
They're not your friends (you were right)
You're means and ends (you're never right)
They're not your friends (and you were right)
It's all pretend (and you were right)

Forgive me fantasy, I pawned you for cheap
To toast your memory with sham pain
Every bubble rises only just to burst
And icy time laughs like a drain
Half lost my way, half found a better man
I've been a man for most my life
I tell myself I'm more than I have done
They'll carve my meat and eat the knife
And you were right

Friends | Who Your Friends Aren't

They're not your friends (you were right)
You're means and ends (you're never right)
They're not your friends (and you were right)
It's all pretend (and you were right)

You know who your friends aren't
You know who not to trust
You might have been golden
But that's turned to dust
But you get the last laugh
'Cause you were right

They're not your friends (you were right)
You're means and ends (you're never right)
They're not your friends (and you were right)
It's all pretend (and you were right)
And you were right
I'm not your friend (you were right)
I'm means to ends (I never fight)
They're not my friends (and you were right)
It's all pretend (and I was right)

Peter Kelly – vocals, guitars
Stuart MacLeod – tambourine
Julia Doogan – vocal

SOME SONGS HAVE TEETH. Those are the ones that tear out of you like dogs chasing rabbits. The most bitter of these tend not to rage as much as they simmer.

Waking from the dream of people being kind is cruel. We waste so much of our time feeling paranoid about what others really think of us that we become uncertain approximations of our true selves.

When the focus is sharpened on the view of your life, it becomes horribly clear that the truth is you seldom pass through the minds of the people around you at all. At best, your place in their thoughts is tantamount to being an apologetic pedestrian holding them up at traffic lights, and some would sooner mow you down than wait for you to cross. At worst, you just aren't there. A ghost who doesn't know they're dead.

———

Who Your Friends Aren't

STUCK AT TRAFFIC LIGHTS on the way to pick Anne up, Caren found herself thinking about that sign above the shop in the main street across the road from her flat. 'Friends Convenience Store'. Those words are often linked – 'friends' and 'convenience' – but we don't usually admit that truth out loud. Picture that. A store where you could buy yourself some convenient friends. Friends at your convenience.

Caren considered herself to be, officially, a good friend. She believed this was how people would generally describe her. In fact, she prided herself on it, almost like she was an expert at being a good friend. When a co-worker got into a bad state on a night out, she would be the one to leave with them in a taxi to make sure they got home okay.

Anne wasn't her friend, not a friend exactly, but that didn't stop Caren from being a friend to her. When she asked if she could have a lift to work last Monday, she jumped at the chance to be kind. She also said she would be happy to drive her back home again. They didn't live that far from each other, it was only a ten-minute detour each way, and nothing gave her more pleasure than being accommodating and helping people out whenever she could.

She had always believed that at the heart of each person was the potential for good. Whenever people talked ill of others, she would leave the room and busy herself with something else rather than be dragged into the mire of gossip and slander. Wherever the vitriol flowed, she took care not to drink. She felt that people with the loudest voices often had the least good to say about others. For her, kindness was not a commodity to be earned, it was free for all and without exception.

Anne got into the car with not so much as a 'good morning'. Caren assumed that she must have had something on her mind and that maybe she would rather not speak about it. She told herself that a good friend would accept this and not take it personally. After all, we all have moments in our day which we must reserve for ourselves and maybe, she thought, this time was one such moment for her.

Normality resumed once they arrived at work and the ice thawed. Conversation flowed as much as it usually did with pedestrian talk of weather and the more professional flavour of communication, like dates for diaries and tasks to populate to-do lists. All fine. All as before. All as expected.

"Same again tomorrow?" Anne asked as they parted for the evening.

"Of course, no problem!" exhaled Caren in a breathless gust of amiable enthusiasm. Another opportunity to be the great friend she knew herself to be. Another chance to enjoy the rush of her own benevolence.

On arriving at her flat the next morning, she found Anne standing with a small companion. Her six-year old daughter. Apart from the strawberry-shaped birthmark on her cheek, she was more or less the common-or-garden pigtailed schoolgirl you are probably visualising.

"You don't mind us dropping Sarah off at school, do you? Only I'm running late this morning and it's not so far out of our way."

"No, no, of course! It's my pleasure," said Caren. "Come on in."

The child sneezed on Caren's ear as she climbed in behind her. When she drove off, a pulsating beat began at the base of her spine – the girl's legs swinging one and then the other into her back.

Again, Anne was dead silent and said not a word until they arrived at the school. She told Caren she wouldn't be a minute and disappeared with Sarah, hand in hand.

Left alone in the car, she caught a glimpse of the dark expression that had appeared on her face in the rear view mirror and at first she didn't recognise herself. With a shock, she corrected it and resumed her placid smile, ready for Anne's return. When she reentered the car, no thanks or further explanation followed, she just sat back in her seat and began swiping and prodding at her phone.

From that day on, this became a daily routine. Caren would pick Anne and Sarah up at their door, drive to the school and then on to work. Approximately the same itinerary ran in reverse later in the day via Anne's mother's house. She would collect Sarah and drive them both home before returning to her own house where she would eat dinner alone, watch television alone and go to bed. Alone.

Caren lived in a large house for someone on their own. She had inherited it from her grandmother, the kindest person she had ever known, and each act of unconditional and seemingly endless goodwill was carried out in tribute to her altruism.

At the end of each night, the wooden floors would echo her solitary footsteps as she made her way across the hall to the spare room to pedal her exercise bike before drifting upstairs to sleep. Those echoes were like italics emphasising that she was definitely alone and at times, she had to admit, they taunted her. She would have liked to have shared this house with someone special but those shoes had so far never been filled. For now, hers were the only footsteps that would announce themselves to these floors. For now, and probably forever.

As time went on, Caren was called upon more and more frequently to drive Anne to pick up late-night shopping if, for example, it was discovered that there was no milk in the fridge for the morning. She would drive over to the flat and text Anne to let her know she was outside. Anne's eldest child, Jennifer, was fourteen and would look after Sarah until they returned.

One night around eleven, as she was preparing to go to bed, Caren heard her mobile cry out from her bedroom. Pausing for a moment, she looked at herself pityingly in the bathroom mirror, her toothbrush hanging ridiculously out of her mouth, before she spat out the toothpaste and dutifully rushed to answer before it stopped. As the tone pulsed on the bedside table, she felt there was a different alarm ringing inside of her. She knew before she looked at the screen who would be calling.

Anne needed a lift. She sounded drunk, her voice wobbling like an overfilled bucket. Caren looked down at her pyjamas and hesistated for a few seconds before reminding herself of what a friend would do.

Ten minutes later, Caren pulled up outside the flat and Anne staggered from the pavement, handbag swinging like a wrecking ball at her side. She steadied herself with the door handle. Her wild eyes struggled to focus and her fingers flicked and gestured for Caren to go, drive, go.

"But where are we going?" Caren asked.

Anne slurred.

"Jackson Street?"

She nodded.

Jackson Street is where the money lives. There stand the big old houses with high ceilings. Two cars in each drive. Land enough that two more houses could be built in the gardens. The people there walk taller and cast bigger shadows. The children in those houses grow up believing they are born for more and they are probably right.

As Caren turned the corner onto Jackson Street, Anne threw out her hand to the wheel, pulling the vehicle to the kerb, forcing Caren to slam the brakes. Anne burst out of the car, tottering towards the driveway of the first house in the street. She dug one quivering hand into her bag as she stumbled in the direction of the door.

Horrified, Caren watched open-mouthed as she threw her other free hand straight through the glass panel at the side of the door and turned the handle on the inside, opening it wide and walking directly into the hall. The last thing she saw before tearing off down the street was Anne drawing the knife and rushing towards a man with terrified eyes that were swollen like birthday balloons.

She didn't wait to see what happened next. She threw her foot down with such force that she felt the stab of the pedal plunge deep into her sole. As she raced into the main street, the store turned its sign from open to closed and, for a few hours at least, friends could neither be bought or sold.

Buttons | *Beyond the Cave*

Buttons

Our buttons pull closed our coats
Most sink but ours always float
'Cause our home is built on flesh and bone
Hours vanish down the sides of our wrists
Magpies dress the walls of our nest
'Cause we sold the things that kill the soul.

Our red thread knots the heart to the head
It's the twine that binds our lives
Flowers that bled are blooming instead
You were always on my mind
You are always on my mind
Like the button you seek but can't find.

Unburdened of the ties round the throats
Folds make our family float
'Cause our gold has no guilt at all.

Our red thread knots the heart to the head
It's the twine that binds our lives
Flowers that bled are blooming instead
You were always on my mind
You are always on my mind
Like the button you dream with at night.

We're sewn like a blanket of snow
We're the movement below the waves
We're stone growing out of the core
We're the light from beyond the cave.

Our red thread knots the heart to the head
It's the twine that binds our lives
Flowers that bled are blooming instead
You were always on my mind
You are always on my mind
Like the button you seek but can't find.

We're sewn like a blanket of snow
We're the movement below the waves
We're stone growing out of the core
We're the light from beyond the cave.
We're sewn like a blanket of snow
We're the movement below the waves
We're stone growing out of the core
We're the light from beyond the cave
Like the button that's lost when it's saved.

Peter Kelly – guitars, mandolin, vocals, foot stomp
Julia Doogan – tambourine
Stuart MacLeod – vocal harmony

NORMALITY IS BEAUTIFUL. The everyday wonder that comes
from the love of a home – the laughter and life of a
family – is spectacular.

It's easy to be distracted by the outside world, driven away
from the truth of your home.

There is no moment more special than the one you pause for.
Possibility lives in that breath. Don't treasure that breath because
it could be your last, treasure it because it might be your first.

Feel the cold and love it. Live in each moment of pain, those
are your teachers. There are no good or bad times,
there's only time.

We don't stop enough. We don't stop to look.

———

Beyond the Cave

I REMEMBER WALKING THROUGH a busy city centre and seeing a man approaching me being hit on the head by a seagull.

Since then, birds have cast a frightening shadow. I salute all magpies in deference, and admittedly through irrational fear, a superstition which my children have inherited. It's an action no-one would instinctively make if they hadn't been told to or heard anything about luck. After you hear that, you have a choice: you become one of those superstitious types or you don't. For other birds, I've never come up with a solution for the fear, I always just quicken my pace and hope for the best.

All fear is irrational, of course. If something is frightening enough to scare you, it's already won. And no fear wins more than the fear of missing out. The truth is that you don't need anything more than to be with the people you love and who love you. That should be a comfort but think of the amount of time you spend purposely denying yourself of their company. We might claim that the world deprives us of that togetherness due to the pressures of work, and whatever else we blame our aloofness on, but that's not it at all. Fear of needing each other pulls us apart. If we believe we are individuals independent of others, even the ones we love, we can convince ourselves that we're strong, we're capable, we're our own people. But no-one is. And no-one owns people. We definitely don't own ourselves.

The birds came on a Wednesday afternoon.

I had just arrived home from work and I found that I had the house to myself. I knew the family would be due in any time so with precious minutes alone, I decided to rest after the trials of my day. Not for the first time, I had been forced to cover for an incompetent and unreliable employee who had failed to arrive for a very important meeting. Repeated calls had been ignored and it seemed he had simply disappeared, leaving others to fend for him, as usual.

The first bird appeared at the window as I prepared to lie down for five, maybe ten minutes. A seagull. It tapped its beak very precisely twice on the window and stopped, as if waiting for me to reply. I closed the curtains and tried to clear any thought of the bird from my head. Lying back on the bed, I shut my eyes.

But I just couldn't switch off. Looking again, I could see its silhouette through the curtain. The tap returned. In some way, it unnerved me even more with its appearance concealed, a veiled assassin.

There was another echo of the first bird's tapping, a stuttering rat-a-tat on the glass like a drum roll before an acrobatic stunt. The shadows told me that there were now at least three, maybe four large gulls on the sill. Rising in a rage, I threw open the curtains, bumping my fists against the window and yelling at the birds to leave me alone. They didn't stir at all and kept on with their tapping, squawking at me as if in uproarious laughter. Furious, I gripped the handle and turned it to open the window wide, expecting the seagulls to flee in shock. Instead, one after another, they burst into the room and encircled me. More and more birds appeared, until the room was a bustle of white feathers and terrible jabbing beaks. A flock of nightmares like Christmas lights caught fire.

I writhed in agony and felt every muscle in me weep as I strained against the collective might of the birds. I screamed and hollered, I cried and moaned, and then eventually gave up all protest. It was no use, they had me, each beak fixed, vice-like, gripping my arms and legs. Truthfully, there was some relief in simply giving in and allowing them to lift me out of the window and into the air.

Whilst I was terrified at what was happening, I couldn't help feeling exhilarated by the experience of being carried higher and higher above the streets where I lived. I was lifted over the town and then further out to the fields, and then on into the distant and alien parts I had never had cause to explore. At this moment, I realised that I had never really experienced freedom before, hemmed into a routine of work-responsibility-sleep, but now I felt that I understood what it meant to be unshackled and alive. Surrounded by birds, I was like a bird. To see birds flying together had always chilled me to the bone. The rhythm of their wings, beating in unity, and their communal purpose unnerved me as someone who could never completely surrender to be with others.

Just as I had begun to enjoy the weightlessness and trust the birds, I confess I felt disappointed when I saw familiar sights return to view once again. As we descended and neared my house, I wished that they would hold me for a little longer, in fact, I even tried to steer them with a turn of my body. The window was still opened wide on its hinges and I assumed that the birds would simply fly me straight back inside.

A man appeared at the window. A man who looked very much like me. A man so identical to me that he could have been my twin. As we got closer, the window seemed more like a mirror. He bore my likeness in every way, from his facial features and posture to his clothes and even the movement of his arm as he closed the window. The birds continued to fly me towards the glass and my screams did nothing to halt them or draw the attention of my doppelgänger, who was now walking away, deeper into the house.

I collided bluntly with the glass and the birds flew off, over the roof and into the clouds.

I managed to grip onto the hood overhanging the window and steadied myself on the ledge. Through the glass, I could hear the muffled voices of my children, and they were unmistakably my children. My boy, my girl. Immediately, I was plunged into a labyrinth of memories: hyperactive birthday parties in cacophonous soft play areas, disrupted nights of illness, bleary-eyed Christmas mornings, tsunamis at bath time. All were reimagined with a pang of longing so powerful that I almost fell off the ledge on which I was perched. I beat my fists on the window and called their names over and over. Their voices continued to shriek and holler, but mine seemed only to exist in some other dimension. I just couldn't connect with them.

Parenthood is bizarre and dizzying. It's strange to think that those lives that stem from your own continue independently, and increasingly in a state of mystery that you only see in snapshots as they get older. There they are, living away and creating their own paths as much more than offshoots of your existence. We're all floating in space and our children are floating in their own space.

Next I saw my wife, busy with arms full of washing and calling out bath-time instructions to the children. She looked capable. Focused. Beautiful. She always does. She always did. I tried calling out her name but before I opened my mouth, I knew that she would not hear me.

Without knowing why, I tried screaming my own name.

"Paul!"

To my horror, this did elicit a response. The man returned to the window. He appeared to look right through me as if he couldn't see I was there. He shrugged and closed the curtains. When the birds returned, I expected they would pick me up in their beaks and carry me away again. But they didn't. They just flew past in their perfect unity. It felt like a mockery as I balanced there on the ledge, face pressed against the glass.

I'm still holding on. I've been here for days now. Maybe my five or ten minutes alone will last forever. I'll hang on here for as long as I can, looking upon that family in that house and that man who enjoys the happiness I didn't stop to realise was mine.

Think of all the minutes spent searching for keys before you can leave your house. Think of all the hours they become. Now think of what that time is telling you and let your island become an 'us' land.

Take it from me – you have everything you need right there where you are. There's a permanence in family. Those networks of threads that over and over again announce the message that we are the same. A family is an echo so massive that the original sound becomes unimaginably small and insignificant, as will be the final sound: unimaginably small and insignificant.

Tiny Graces | *The Belly of the Whale*

Tiny Graces

There's an art to living well that's not revenge
Arm the anger with an anchor and keep your head
Tie the laces of the shoes that take you places far from blues
Be an army for your love and pledge your truth.
We'll build an ark with hands in hands, not wood and nails
Calm the storm with gentle breaths and soft details
Tidal races will whirlpool but no wave will dare touch you
Be an army for your love, you're bulletproof.

If you're a secret no-one can tell
You're just the sea deaf in the shell
You've been trying to no avail
To keep the tide behind a veil
You tend towards the swell
You have a thirst that none can quell
Resigned to live inside the belly of the whale.

If the sharks smell blood they'll circle what they crave
But a lamb can be wolf and courage will be saved
Tiny graces fall on you and cause the flowers onboard to bloom
Be an army for your love and live as proof.

If you're a secret no-one can tell
You're just the sea deaf in the shell
You've been sinking since you set sail
So now it's unnatural not to fail
You tend towards the swell
You have a thirst that none can quell
Resigned to live inside the belly of the whale.
If you're a secret no-one can tell
You're just the sea deaf in the shell
You've been trying to no avail
To keep the tide behind a veil
You tend towards the swell
You have a thirst that none can quell
Resigned to live inside the belly of the whale
Resigned to live inside the belly of the whale

Peter Kelly – vocal, guitar

WE ALL KNOW AND HATE the limits that impose on our freedom.

In every life, the cage takes a different shape, the only constant amongst all lives is its existence in one form or another.

We dream of how life would be without that thing which casts a permanent shadow and fantasise about a happiness eternally out of reach. Hungry for perfection, we starve ourselves of the satisfaction of acceptance.

We all feel sure that there is more, when all there is is now.

You won.

The cure for this malady is to love your limits and celebrate everything in your life, good and bad. All parts of the jigsaw make a perfect picture.

———

The Belly of the Whale

I HAVE COME TO REALISE that to be happy, you have to be happy right now. If your happiness only exists in the future, then it doesn't really exist at all. It's so sad that no-one ever seems to be quite where they want to be and no-one is ever even really where they are for more than a moment. They're always imagining themselves out of where they are. Imagining themselves somewhere better. Imagining themselves someone better.

Resentment eats at you all day until one day, it's just eaten you. The writer becomes the book that tears out its own pages. It makes me think of Jonah and the whale. Picture living inside your bitterness as if it was a whale.

Anger ties a knot in your throat. Every word you speak must travel first past that knot, negotiating all the pain and resentment that leaves you barely able to breathe. Nothing you swallow goes down without discomfort. Many people spend every day hiding their rage, perhaps directed at one person, perhaps aimed at the whole world. It's a wonder we don't all break out fighting in the streets.

Maybe one day we will. Then it might be that only one person is left standing. One person immune to animosity, standing there surrounded by the fallen, everyone having offed each other in the ultimate consummation of rage. It was on one of those days when bitterness was eating me for dinner that I discovered the poisonous, magical power of my thoughts.

Friday morning had arrived abruptly after another night of cruel insomnia. The shrieking of my bedside alarm clock dragged me out of a shallow, brittle sleep. 6.30. Light spilled in through the spaces between the curtains and my bedroom window. For around a week and a half, I had managed no more than three hours a night and I was really beginning to fear for my threadbare sanity. It's well known that there is only so long you can go without rest, and I was especially distressed at my out-of-character sleeplessness having never had trouble turning off before. Every time I closed my eyes to attempt to sleep, my imagination would instantly animate chaotic and horrifying scenes that brought me crashing back to reality with a shocking start.

The shrill screech of the alarm tone droned and repeated, droned and repeated.

I stared at the LED numbers, taunting me with their demonic red. I imagined them retreating and reversing to allow me more time to rest, any time at all. In my exhaustion, I felt myself becoming transfixed by the luminous digits and the bars that formed their shapes on the display. The act of focusing was entrancing and I began to feel as if I was actually inside of the numbers, as if I could touch the walls that gave them their structure. I reached out my hands, and sure enough, the bars were solid. With some effort, I found I was able to switch them around to form new shapes around me. The energy of the clock pulsed through my veins and I suddenly found that I was no longer tired and no longer scared.

The sound of the alarm had disappeared and the light had gone with it.

The clock now read 3.30. I rubbed my eyes. Still, 3.30. I laughed and shook my head at the thought. It was impossible. Awakening my phone, I checked the time on the display: 3.30. I turned on the television and in the corner of the screen, the news ticker confirmed the time was 3.30. It was 3.30 everywhere, and unfeasible as it seemed, it appeared this had somehow been my doing.

Drunk with excitement, the last thing I could have contemplated doing at this moment was trying to sleep. At first, I felt restless to begin the new day with this fresh sense of power and considered exploring my ability to move time forward as well as back, but I stopped myself from acting on the temptation. For the first time in as long as I could remember, I paused in each moment of the passing hours and noticed the changes of the world as it came to life.

Looking out of the window, I saw people panicked into action, fluttering and flapping to catch up with time. My natural proclivity for mischief led me to throw an abandoned newspaper up from the ground in a gust of wind to land in the face of a man running for his bus. He grabbed at the pages and tossed them to the side as he watched the driver pull away from the stop.

When I left my flat at seven o' clock, I felt as if I was walking around in broad daylight with a loaded gun raised above my head. I felt like the loaded gun was my head itself. There was a thrill and a terror in knowing what my imagination could do. "Step back everyone," I said inside myself. "You don't know who you're messing with." I felt like an actor in the movie of my own life but in this version, everything was real and nothing was real. I was wide awake in a dreamworld, or maybe I was dreaming in the wide awake world.

As I walked down the street, I toyed with my surroundings and with everyone I saw around me. Throwing people in my path out of the way like skittles, stopping cars dead in the road and speeding up the birds in the sky sending them hurtling into shop windows. I changed the traffic lights from green to red and back again, as if orchestrating a light display at a rock concert. I turned up all the volume controls on all of the shop stereos until customers were rushing out of the stores with their hands clasped over their ears. I opened up holes in the road and crowds of people fell straight in as they ran blindly to escape the deafening shop muzak.

For a while that day, I was happier than I have ever been. Having felt pretty powerless for years, I had become omnipotent overnight, and the scope of my control was intoxicating. As a God of my own universe, I felt sure I would never have the need to cast my eyes upward or throw my knees to the floor again.

But soon, the picture saddened me and more than ever, I felt alone, like I suppose a God would feel.

As I watched crowds of people following each other into the holes I had made in the pavements and vehicles tumbling into the chasms in the road, I felt envious of all of those people and things falling together. That togetherness was what I had missed while I was powerless and that togetherness was what I missed now that I was powerful. In the end, I realised that it wasn't weakness that caused me pain, it was being alone.

All day we're defensive. We are under attack from ourselves before anyone else can get a look-in. We tell ourselves that nothing is good enough. We can do better. We must do better. But nothing is bigger than we could ever be. It goes on for infinite miles and infinite seconds and infinite lives. We're right that nothing is enough; nothing will be enough forever. All of our hellos and all of our goodbyes are drowned in that infinity of nothing.

Rather than standing back as a lonely spectator, I threw myself into the scene of devastation I had created. I joined the throng of people that was being magnetically drawn to a massive gaping mouth in the concrete and allowed myself to be swallowed by the chaos. I was elated to realise that there were hundreds more behind me, as well as in front. We were all in it together and I realised that it was this togetherness, and not power, that could bring me happiness. We were an immediate human family. All powerless but together, which made us all-powerful together.

Looking into the void as I felt myself falling, I saw the true horror unfolding ahead of me. As the world tipped upside down, everything appeared once again exactly as it had before.

It was as if nothing had changed at all. There were no holes in the pavements. The roads were intact. Everyone walked and drove towards some destination with a purpose and a certainty that they would arrive. Everyone but me.

Looking behind and around me, I could see no sign of the openings I had made in the ground. I could see no proof of the impact of my power or feel its magic coursing through my body. I could see no sign of any other world than the one in which I now stood. A world where I was powerless. A world in which I was alone.

Afterword | *Songs Last*

It might be a funny thing to ask at the end of a book, but why bother writing anything? It seems that more people write than read now, so who is there to write for? It always was a selfish conceit.

I have a vivid childhood memory of trying to walk through a wall. As a child, you believe that anything is possible. As you get older, you might get wiser but becoming more committed to an idea doesn't necessarily mean being more certain that you're right. Pictorially, a human life might be best illustrated in a comic strip. In the first square, the child is walking through a wall. In the second, the adult is telling the child it can't be done. In the third, the wall collapses on them both.

Adults don't have it all sewn up but they're sewn into the clothes that help them remember who they are. Who they must be. Who they've agreed to be.

As a child, you believe that adults have some sort of power and then you get there and discover the infinitesimal autonomy you enjoy could fit inside a thimble. Look at your life and all the time you occupy looking forward. It's like you're a ghost of the future haunting your present. Responsibilities are hungry and will eat you alive. Your minutes are planned more than they're lived and you exist in a state of eternal frustration, not at having failed to shake yourself free, but at having chosen to remain a prisoner. You're more a boss of your body than a person sometimes.

The more you embrace the adult world, the more you come to resemble other adults. We abandon creativity for necessity, and in doing so, we abandon ourselves.

We perform for others so much of the time that we might even forget that it's a performance, and so we continue to act, even alone, until we become almost unrecognisable to ourselves. Maybe you know the midnight terror that sets in when you meet a stranger in your home, in your own skin.

So that's it there. That's the reason to write. Write because it's your heart. Giving your heart to the world is giving it life. And let them break it. Once you've given it away, it's not yours to protect or preserve. Destruction is creation, or so says Picasso and, well, he's Picasso. So let it happen. Just throw it out to the dogs and let them do what they will. (I'm arguing with myself now to let it go.)

Eventually, there will be the last songs. But songs last. Not just the loved ones but the ones nobody likes, the lonely ones, the ugly ones, and even the forgotten ones. They're all out there for good, floating around in the air like lost balloons. They're breaths, kissed into life. Songs are dreams that escaped. I think that when you dream, you're peeking behind the scenes at the real nature beyond nature. A dream shows you the truth in the way a boom mic does when it floats into the camera shot. There are cracks all over: this egg is hatching soon.

Maybe when you sleep, you don't sleep at all. Maybe the reason your dreams are so real is that you're really always awake. Maybe the line between your imagined world and the world you imagine in is an eyelid, barely open, barely closed.

Thanks:

Stuart MacLeod

Julia Doogan

Neil Wilson

Jason Cranwell

Martin Greig

Charles McGarry

Kristin Hersh